To Ethel:
Sine Te Nihil
Nulli secundus
Ego Ipse Habeo Facto

How Women Saved Civilization

Lollipop's Tale

By Lollipop
A.K.A. Bernard Michael Patten, M.D.

Fellow of the American College of Physicians
Fellow of the Royal Society of Medicine
Fellow of the Texas Neurological Society
Fellow of the American Academy of Neurology
Memory Fellow of the New York Academy of Medicine
Diplomate of the American Board of Psychiatry and Neurology

For permission requests, write to the publisher at:
contact@identitypublications.com.

Ordering Information:
Quantity sales. Special discounts are available on quantity purchases by corporations, associations, and others. For details, contact the publisher at the address above.

Orders by U.S. trade bookstores and wholesalers.
Please contact Identity Publications:
Tel: (805) 259-3724 or visit www.IdentityPublications.com.

ISBN-13: 978-1-945884-72-6 (paperback)
ISBN-13: 978-1-945884-73-3 (hardcover)

First Edition
Publishing by Identity Publications.
www.IdentityPublications.com

TABLE OF CONTENTS

CHAPTER ONE

THE DISCONSOLATE AWAKENING

"In the desert, there is no sign that says: 'Thou shalt not eat stones.'"

—Sufi proverb

Call me Lollipop.

Yes, that's my name, an acquired name based on—oh, I don't know what—personal characteristics, I suppose. I am colorful, usually bright red or green, and I am sweet most times and lickable. And my body is solid, very solid, lithe, and one with me. This book, if you continue to read, will tell you how I used it (my body) and how I used other people to push buttons of one sort or another that made things run and made things happen.

Where did it come from? The name. Where?

Who knows?

Probably one of my boyfriends. Let's see. Abe? Bernard? Carl? Maybe David or Drue, or Daniel? Or how about Ed One or Ed Two? Or was it Fred, George, or Harry? You get the picture. I've been around.

Yeah. I've been around. Picture me in my salad days when I was green in judgment. Picture me in the back seat of some rundown

Plymouth Champion in some semi-deserted parking lot at night, getting licked and slobbered all over by an amateur or, in some cases, by amateurs. All that was part of my real problem, a problem that started when I was a teenager. I worshipped boys, and then I worshipped men. I still do, but not as much as then. When I look at a man, I don't see a human being. I see a god, an Adonis. To me, men are the most delicious thing on this planet. I know this is a personal failing. I can't help it. I love them, and I will love them until I die. And I love what they do to me and how they make me feel, and I love how they smell and how they taste. I love everything about them. There are some guys that don't send me. Why they leave me cold is a question to which there are as many answers as there are women. Clark, for instance, you'll read about him soon, healthy enough and man enough, but he moves me not at all. Why?

Hodge, for instance. Take Hodge. Whenever he walks near me, my knees get weak. If he so much as looked at me, even though his glances seemed impersonal or cold, my heart thumped like a tom-tom. He affects the other girls the same way; they rave about how handsome he is, how hot, how sexy, and what a spiffy dresser. I was not making a play for him. This is different. This is love.

Too bad men have screwed up society so badly that we women had to eliminate them completely, actually change them completely. We had to do it to save ourselves and the planet. About that, more later.

When you are around, you get to know things, lots of stuff that you don't read in books. That's one of the reasons I am writing this—to tell what I learned and also why and how I learned it. So, at last, this info can be found in books. Use it if you want, or don't use it if you don't want. Books are still a source of useful information, unlike the internet or Fox News.

Men are low down, dirty, and deceitful. That's one thing I learned. They want one thing and one thing only. No, retract that last statement. They usually want two things: food and sex, usually in that order. Yes, ladies, it is that simple. Keep it in mind—it is that simple.

After they have eaten to satiety, most men just want to get between your legs. A man is a sex machine and not much more. That's his real purpose in life. Learn how to manipulate them for your own purposes for your own good. Lead them around by the nose. That's a metaphor meaning lead them around by their dicks.

Our new government, Women's World, Lady Land, recognizes men have only one purpose in life: to make more women. With new biological engineering, we now have the power to populate Earth with only women and/or a new type of biologically engineered man. The technique is amazing and amazingly simple, considering what was accomplished with a single biological agent. About that, more later.

Some of you readers out there who are still awake may be wondering how in the world we would use men just to make women. It was easier than you think. Human biology is fundamentally simple. Sperms with a Y move faster and are lighter than those with an X and can be easily separated by the sex sorter centrifuge. The Y sperms get the boot, and the X sperms get to in vitro or in vivo fertilization. The average ejaculate has, I am told, four million sperms. I believe it, although I never counted them myself. That's two million with an X and two million with a Y. We freeze the X sperms and chuck the Y sperms. Now we have from just one ejaculate enough sperms to make by IVF (in vitro fertilization) or IVoF (in vivo fertilization) two million women. Even sperm from dead men can be used and frozen. Thus, through the miracle of biotechnology, we can store enough sperm to repopulate our planet for at least 1,000 years, and even dead men can and will have daughters.

Some men will be kept here on a temporary basis as sex slaves in case something goes wrong with the above-mentioned plan. A mouse is not worth a radish or a redfish if it has but one hole to run to. Always have options. I hope someday we will learn to culture X sperms in test tubes. When that sacred time arrives, the world will be populated only by women forever. That's the final solution, so to speak. The final solution to the gender problem. One gender and one gender only—female. Soon to be nature's way.

Not all men, of course, are low down, dirty, and deceitful. For instance, my Hodge. He is a man and a sex machine and, I might add, an eating machine, but he is also a man in touch with his feminine side. He is not effeminate. No way. He makes nice Grand Marnier souffles and delicious crab imperial. Things like that. He appreciates a well-grown eggplant, and he even likes cats, except he is quite allergic to them.

Hodge is generally sloppy but otherwise okay, more or less controllable, and with a good sense of humor. We have lived together on and off for five years, six months, and 22 days. Most of that was happy, and he helped organize the men to get where we needed to be in the network. Some day we may marry. About that, more later.

Sometimes Hodge and I argue and usually about stupid things like whose turn it is to clean the toilet or rack the dishes, and sometimes we argue about what is important or unimportant. That is our stupidest argument.

Hodge is not what most women would call handsome, but to my heart, he holds the key. He says he is trying to look at women as persons, but it is hard because, to him, they all are goddesses. Yes, goddesses, not sex objects. Sometimes I think he actually believes this, and sometimes I think he doesn't, and sometimes I think he believes it and doesn't believe it at the same time. Hodge says he is not worthy to kiss my feet. Ho ho ho. That sounds good, and that's the way we want the men to be—completely and totally subservient, now and forever, until we eliminate them or change them altogether. Yes, we aimed to eliminate all brutish men, substituting a new brand, a new type of man, but of course, not my Hodge, not my Hodge. He stays the same.

Men like Hodge helped us take control. They were needed, and without them, the movement might have failed. No change that. Without them, the movement would have failed. Later I will show you how they helped and when and where. Meanwhile, let's praise Hodge and the other men. They proved that men are not entirely useless.

Yes, control. Historians will want to know how we women took control, and they (the women historians, of course, because men are not allowed to do history or even read or write—we fixed that) will decide whether it was justified or not justified. That's their problem. My role is clear and was clear. I led the movement, and I led the violence, and I made the decisions. The picture will not be complete until all precincts are heard from. There are aspects of the scene on which I am particularly well qualified to report. Actually, better qualified than anyone now alive.

And, yes, I am a legend in my own time. Okay. Full disclosure: Lollipop is my code name and the name that truly struck fear in the hearts of men once we women got rolling. And Lollipop signed her share of death warrants and executions. Some eliminated the male sex completely. You bet. And I would do it again with pleasure. My real name is Polish, very Polish and hardly pronounceable by most people. Andzelika Dziedzic. The first name means god's messenger, and the last name means land owner. If you can't say it or remember it—no matter. Just call me Lollipop. After I became the supreme leader of the world, I changed my name to Queen Azura after those old Flash Gordon movies. Andzelika, Lollipop, Queen Azura—call me what you wish, and I shall remain the same identical person, more or less.

Ugh! I have to get away from the ego thing and stick to the subject. Stick to the truth so women can stay in charge and can keep calling the shots. I do tend to be discursive, writing like most people think, and I will try to control such in the pages that follow. It's hard for me and for most women. We like to talk, and most times, we talk too much.

About the movement.

Ho ho ho. That is not the right word for what we did and how it happened that the world is now much, much better off (but still not perfect) than it had been when the men ran things. Movement is wrong. Movement as in women's movement—that's not what we did. It's bad diction. Misleading and incorrect. And it was not an insurrection. No! Not a revoke and not a revocation. Not a revolution either. Certainly not a movement in the usual sense. Nope, none of that. No way. I would say it was an avulsion. Yes, we avulsed men from power. That was the only way. They would have hung on and on and on unless we avulsed them. We ended their long and disastrous control of things. We cut them off brutally. We deposited the mighty from their seats and exalted those of low degree. We effectively made amends for hundreds of heroic centuries when we bore the burdens literally as if we were their slaves and they were the slave masters. We avenged the horrible deaths inflicted on women through the centuries, including the millions of our sisters burned at the stake, accused and convicted of witchcraft.

Avulsion 1. The action of pulling off, plucking out, or tearing away, forcible separation.

Oxford English Dictionary Second Edition, v3.1

If I sound bitter, it is because I am bitter, very bitter. Most of us were bitter, and those of us women who were not bitter should have been.

Sure, some of the good guys suffered during the transition, including my Hodge. He went to Spec's to buy some of the Jefferson Ocean. That's a bourbon whiskey he loves. I almost said he lives for. It's called Ocean because they put the bourbon in oak casks that have been charred on the inside and then put the casks on ocean-going cargo ships that visit the seven seas. The motion of the ocean causes the bourbon to wash against the charcoal, and the charcoal removes ketones and aldehydes, making a smoother drink altogether.

We, women, had abolished cash and money, as it used to be known. Money no longer existed. On Erasure Day (now a national holiday), what was money just became digital entries in some computer bank. Ledger entries and nothing else gave us complete control of finance. Where was I?

Oh yeah, Hodge. He presented his plastic, and the Compustat flashed a red light, and a dull voice announced in computer monotones: Not approved. The clerk, at Hodge's insistence, ran the card again. Again no, no dice. When he arrived home, he still thought it was some kind of computer quirk. He called Mike, and Mike had the same problem. In fact, all men had the same problem. They had to have the same problem because that is the way we fixed it.

Pulling a few of the right switches, we disabled all accounts that were listed under the title "sex male or male or male sex." Easy as pie. We got the idea from the way the United Snakes of America blocked the accounts of all those Russian oligarchs. Press a few buttons and swish—the money disappears. Even money in Swiss bank accounts. What they thought they had, they no longer had. Men no longer needed money, anyway, because we women took charge of all the getting and spending. This stroke was to make up for centuries when men controlled finance, the Federal Reserve Bank, the stock markets, international trade, the courts, the congress, most major corporations, and so forth. Men controlled almost everything. It wasn't right, and it wasn't fair, so we fixed it.

At first, Hodge and the others didn't like what was what. Who could blame them? But after a while, they acquiesced. What else could they do? Nothing. We had them by the balls, so to speak. We had them where we wanted them, and they can't escape no how. Detailed study and careful planning paid off in big dividends.

Question: So why is this chapter entitled disconsolate enlightenment?

Answer: Because it deals with how all this came about, my enlightenment, which was unhappy, uncomfortable, comfortless, and forlorn. Like the Buddha, I suddenly understood. I wasn't being driven around by my charioteer Chandaka, and I didn't see an old man, and I didn't learn that people grow old and get sick and die. Crap like that. Nor did my enlightenment happen under the Mahabodhi Tree. Nope, it came via the internet with the news that the Extreme Court of the United States had voted 5 to 4 to abolish the freedom of 66 million women to decide what to do with their bodies. Outrageous!

The right-wing religious bastards took away freedoms our mothers and grandmothers enjoyed. Yesterday, June 25, 2022, a day that will live in infamy, the radical right reversed Roe versus Wade. And that was the tipping point. That was the tipping point (or is the right word *tripping point*?) that pushed me and us and the majority of women into the avulsion mode. Forcing women to carry a pregnancy against their will is dangerous. It poses high health risks, makes it harder to escape poverty, can derail education, career, and life plans, and makes it difficult to leave an abusive partner. With federal protections erased, those who suffer pregnancy losses like a natural miscarriage could be and, I predicted, would be subject to suspicion, investigation, and arrest. Patients and the doctors who care for them could be thrown in jail.

Enough is enough! Nothing short of war can stop this outrage. I resolved to steel up myself and others for war, war against men. We channeled and will channel our anger into action.

The key to the avulsion was to copy their methods, the methods men used to gain power. That was the original plan. Human nature hasn't changed much in the last 8,000 years. People in power like to keep it that way. We needed to know how men gained control and how they kept it.

The Extreme Court reversed two previous rulings. Lesson: When you want to push for control, the past counts for nothing. If the Extreme Court could ignore their own previous legal decisions, so can we. We do but sing after them and follow their lead.

The Extreme Court used lots of legalese to justify the oppression. Lesson: Do the same. Quote the Declaration of Independence, which says we are entitled to life, liberty, and the pursuit of happiness, and if we don't get it, it is the right of the people, our right, to abolish such government and institute new guards for future security and happiness. All this is right there in print for us to use. If the Extreme Court can use printed bullshit to justify anything they feel like doing, so can we. You agree?

The Extreme Court viewed issues through the religious lens. Lesson: Do the same. But right now, I can't think of how to do that. Religion is easily used, was easily used to oppress women and slaves. How to turn it around will require work, lots of work. And time. And energy and new ideas about what is religious and what is not. Maybe we can go back to the worship of goddesses like Rhea, Cybele, Britta, Bridgit, Dagda, Diana, Isis, Juno, Anuket, Nerthus, Selene, Andraste, Anarnod, Tanit, Hathor, Modron, Blodedneed, and Maat, goddess of truth and justice. How about Mut, the lioness goddess of Karnak, or Opet, a grandly pregnant hippo goddess who could contain and protect new life? What about Hathor, a gentle cow goddess who represented sexualized beauty incarnate at her temple at Dendera, and so forth? It had worked for centuries. It might work again. We might make a new religion based on compassion and sympathy. We might make a new religion where the main god is a woman and not a man. God the Mother, instead of God the Father. Confession could start: "Bless me, Mother, for I have sinned." And the person hearing the confession would be a woman, a priestess.

To paraphrase the Declaration: When a long train of abuses and usurpations, pursuing invariably the same object, evinces in them a design to reduce them under absolute despotism, it is their right, it is their duty, to throw off such government and to provide new guards for their future security and happiness.

Pretty clear. Right?

My point is if the Extreme Court can use bullshit and legalese to justify their position, so can we. The Extreme Court now views issues in every situation through the narrow lens of religion. And because of that, 66 million women in 25 states lost the absolute freedom to control an important part of their lives and their bodies—pregnancy.

The Extreme Court reversed the Roe v. Wade decision (I am not making this up) by a 5-to-4 vote. Lesson: Even a one-vote majority can seize or control power. Since women are 51.2% of the humans in this fair country and 51.6% of the voters, we have the absolute right as the majority to seize absolute power, just as the Extreme Court assumes it had an absolute right to seize power and call the shots about our bodies by the thinnest of a majority, one fucking vote!

So, what's the point? The point is we should study what men did to get power, and we should copy them. We should use the lessons of contemporary civilization to construct our own society and civilization. We were not pro-abortion nor against it. If a woman does not want an abortion, we think she shouldn't get it. If a woman does want an abortion, we think she should be permitted to get it. It's not a matter of abortion or no abortion; it is a matter of personal freedom to decide for oneself.

Woman's World. It just won't happen on its own. We needed to know tactics and strategy and networking and organization and finance and weapons, especially weapons—powerful weapons, a whole bunch of other things. History too. We had to learn how men got and kept control so we could copy them and do the same. That meant I needed to go back to school to study and learn. The mission was clear. The methods would have to come from deep thinking and serious work in libraries and in college courses.

The first course I took, *Why Women Should Rule the World*, was at a small community college called San Jacinto Junior in, of all places, Pasadena, Texas. The professor was Dante Mephistopheles. That's his name, all right. But what's in a name, says Shakespeare. A rose by any other name would smell as sweet. If I were he, I would have changed my name. But I am not he, and it turned out his name did reflect aspects of his character—part poet and part you-know-what.

CHAPTER TWO

WHY WOMEN SHOULD RULE THE WORLD, 101, FOUR CREDITS, LIMITED ENROLLMENT, TERM PAPERS, AND BOOK REVIEWS REQUIRED

"Nolite te bastardes carborundorum."

—English schoolboy slogan in fake Latin meaning
"Don't let the bastards grind you down."

Professor Meph-foe (that's what we call him) was right out of central casting—urbane, articulate, humorous, witty, gracious, and well-dressed in a pin-striped charcoal Brooks Brothers three-piece suit, the kind that went out of fashion decades ago. He stood 5'10" and was slightly stooped. For some reason, his face was very pale, almost ghostly white. Ditto his arms. Probably he spends too much time indoors and lacks a tan, or he might have had one of those face peels that leaves people ghostly white, but face peel wouldn't explain the arm pallor.

Meph-foe's knowledge was vast and deep. Rumor had it he was a Brahmin, the intellectual priest caste, the highest caste of the four varnas. He definitely looked like nobility, in this case, nobility from the Indian subcontinent.

One wondered why he was teaching at a Junior College and not at Columbia or Harvard or Brown, or some other Ivy League University. Probably he had gotten into trouble. Probably something sexual, I would say. He looked the type. It's in the eyes and in the wan wistful smile. I told you I'd been around. I can spot them a mile away. Men on the make. He was one of them and looked the part.

Meph-foe had enchanting anecdotes up his sleeve for every topic and every question and occasion. He could explain anything and everything with facts and details in the charming turn of a phase and a certain originality that was his hallmark. He was also discursive in an interesting sort of way that was never boring.

With his white mustache, white beard, and silver hair (why pretend you are not old?), all us women students found him charming and distinguished. That, of course, was the desired effect—what he was looking for, working for, leering for, aching for, and lusting for.

"I know lots of things you don't know," he said. "Lots of things. I have read many books. Many books. I have seen the world. Seen many places that you all can't even locate on a map. And history. I know history, more history than you will ever know. Ever know. History is key. History is key. Real key. Those who don't learn history are doomed to repeat it. The quote is likely due to Harvard writer and philosopher George Santayana, and in its original form, it read, 'Those who cannot remember the past are condemned to repeat it.' Edmund Burke famously said the same. I say those who don't know history and those who do know history are both doomed to repeat it. Perhaps the greatest lesson of history is that we never learn from history. But that doesn't mean we can't try."

"Although I am in the philosophy department, ethics division, this course will be mainly about politics, female politics, and female power and why and how men have screwed up badly. Screwed up badly. That is what you signed up for, and that is what you are going to get."

Note to reader: Meph-foe was speaking truer than he knew, as subsequent events proved.

We two hundred students, the maximum allowed, 199 women, all in our late teens or early twenties except for me and one fairly ancient woman named Gertrude Smith, who looked way over the hill. We students all sat in silent reverence, immortalizing Meph-foe's every phrase with our pads and pens. You bet our lecture hall was highly estrogenized. What did you expect, considering the course title? Correction: We were in the music auditorium on the north side of campus. It became our lecture hall because there was no other place to accommodate our numbers.

Besides the one male student, Hodge (this class is where I met him) and Meph-foe, there always was another male in the room who sat on the left side of the green board at the right hand of Meph-foe. He looked like what used to be called white trash. About the mid or late twenties, thick blond hair, short stature, I'd say about five two in his stocking feet, and with a really rather brutal face with a nose that had been punched crooked and a scar down his right cheek. Obviously, he looked too dumb and too beaten down to be a graduate student. Probably had been an abused child by an alcoholic father and grew up in an RV park or a run-down flat in a tenement slum or an orphanage for abandoned children.

This man's job was to help with the housekeeping, distribute the quizzes, hand back the papers Meph-foe had graded, work the projector for the power point, and so forth. A regular gopher. But Lorrie told me she had seen Clark and Meph-foe arm and arm in the hallway. "Too sweet," said Lorrie. "Both of them too sweet."

I wonder. These days anything goes. You never know. By the way, Lorrie is stacked, so we others are jealous. Our jealousy is fueled further by her wearing a micromini dress and her wiggle when she walks, the trail of perfume that follows her, and her giggle when she talks. High black stiletto high heels make her look taller and raise her butt, making her look younger and slutty. Men hang around her the way flies hang around honey. Life is cruel, especially for us flat-chested.

A fuss at the podium. Flatting his hands on the wooden surface and addressing us directly, with a grave nod of his magnificent head of white hair, Meph-foe continued.

"They say travel broadens the mind. Broadens the mind. No doubt it does. Clark, slides please."

Clark hit the lights, pressed a button that lowered the silver screen obscuring the green board, and went to the back of the room to work the projector.

What followed was a series of travel scenes, most of which showed Meph-foe and some of which showed Meph-foe with Clark. I made careful notes just in case some of this stuff might show up on the next test or quiz. Truth be told, I hadn't realized travel could be so interesting. The slides and commentary were first-class."

Egypt: "When the long-lived King Djer died, sacrificial burials took place at Abydos where 587 were killed to accompany the king to the afterlife, not to mention unimaginable wealth and commodities for the king's consumption. Similar ritual murders have been uncovered in the north at Saqqara (62 souls and some dogs to accompany their master), the capital of Egypt at the time. Killing that many people can't have been easy and was probably not accomplished in a single day. There were no bullets, no guillotine to speed the process—just the standard ancient methods of strangulation, poison, and blood-letting. About 85% of the dead surrounding the tomb of Djer—at least of those for whom markers could be read or bodies identified—belonged, you guessed it, to young and healthy women, two of whom were identified as queens. These burials and many more like them were the product of fervent religious beliefs. Religion gave the king an ideological chokehold on the people. This was a time of unchecked male power."

Meph-foe paused, looked around the room to see if his words had had impact, smiled, nodded, and then said, "Next slide, Clark."

"Here we experience treasures of the Mekong River from aboard the intimate 12-suite 'Mekong Princess,' stopping to explore destinations virtually unknown to travelers in China. Clark and I played Mahjong with two tour guides and lost our shirts."

"Here, we explore the wilds of the Galapagos, an island off the coast of Ecuador where animals never learned to fear mankind. Clark and I actually swam and played with baby seals and sea lions while their mothers looked on and smiled."

"Look at the lovely verdant rural landscapes of Colima and Oaxaca, where indigenous roots are still strong. Examine the imposing Mayan ruins of Palenque and Chichen Itza. The ballcourt game was deadly serious, with the losers ritualistically executed. And when it didn't rain enough, and the corn crop failed, young women were adorned with gold and jewels and thrown into the cenote to appease Tlaloc, the rain god. Maya writing has recently been translated and reveals the same awful history of war and brutality, always sponsored by men, all the gory details similar to that of Asia, Europe, and every other place that left records, proving the Maya were never the peaceful, fun-loving people that we had thought."

A woman in back on my left shouted, "How do we know that for sure? I thought no one had been able to translate Maya writing."

Good for her. It is about time some of the ladies spoke up and showed they were still alive."

Meph-foe had a pained expression on his face and shook his head. "My God, we do get sidetracked in this course. It took the concerted efforts of three individuals to crack the Maya writing system: an Englishman, Sir Eric Thompson, a Ukrainian scholar named Yuri Knorosov, and a Russian, Tatiana Proskouriakoff. The breakthrough came by reading texts by Bishop Diego de Landa. Although Landa's own understanding of Maya writing was misguided, his manuscript served as an essential key for Knorosov."

"Next slide, Clark."

"Here, we ventured off the beaten path to experience hidden gems of history in the high Andes where prepubescent girls were murdered, probably for some religious reason, and their bodies left frozen on the mountaintops for the benefit of the gods. Modern archeologists are trying to figure out what was what that led to these terrible murders. Did the kids volunteer to die? Who knows?"

"In 1995, anthropologist John Reinhard found a mummy of a 12-to-14-old Inca female on mount Ampato in Peru."

"Her picture, Clark."

"She is called the Ice Maiden or Juanita. She had been buried for over 500 years and was probably an Inca sacrifice. It is estimated there are hundreds of Inca children encased in what are now ice tombs on top of peaks in the Andes where there are over 115 known Inca ceremonial sites."

"Yes, Hodge."

"Sir, you don't know why they sacrificed girls. There may have been many other reasons than their sex. Maybe the gods themselves preferred girls."

"Hodge, the gods don't exist. The men who ran the Inca show decided who gets killed and who doesn't. I think the reason there are girls is men were in charge of the society and the religion. For the same reason, there are no altar girls, only altar boys, no female popes, and no female Dalai Lamas—clerical misogyny that in Western culture started in the fourth century and continues throughout the world to the present. The great Catholic Church still has no women priestesses. Ancient Greece and ancient Rome had many. For the same reason, there are few varsity sports for women in American high schools. The girls have cheerleading and maybe band, color guard, and that's it."

"Excuse me, sir. The Catholic Church has had altar girls since 1996 if the Bishop gives permission."

"What's your name?"

"Susan, sir, with respect. Susan Granger."

"Susan, are you a Catholic?"

"Yes, sir."

"Susan, do you go to mass every Sunday?"

"Yes, I do."

"How about on Holy Days of Obligation? Do you go to mass?"

"Always."

"Have you, in all the times you have gone to mass, ever seen an actual altar girl?"

"No, sir, I haven't. But that doesn't mean they don't exist."

"Have you ever seen a ghost?"

"No."

"Does that mean ghosts exist?"

"No, it doesn't. But it doesn't prove ghosts don't exist."

"Susan, if you see it, believe it. If you don't see it, you don't know. Would it be fair to say that altar girls exist in theory, but in practice, we have no information about whether they exist or not? If you ever see a real live altar girl, let me know. Meanwhile, I think there are very few altar girls, and perhaps there are none.

 "Next slide."

"Clark and I hiked long and hard to find the Darwin's frog, one of the several unique species endemic to northern Patagonia. Look at the beautiful bright green back and the jet fiery red front of this marvelous creature. This endangered forest denizen named for you-know-who has an unusual way of raising its young. The male carries the growing embryos in his vocal sack until they are tadpoles ready to emerge."

"This is the Convento of San Pedro Claver that marks the southern perimeter of El Centro, the old section of Cartagena, Colombia. Claver (1580-1654), a Jesuit known as the slave of the slaves, devoted his life to the Africans brought in bondage to Cartagena. His skeleton lies there in a glass case under the main altar. We have a picture from the guidebook. There—see how well-preserved he is!"

"While we were looking, a beautiful woman in a tight dress and a good decolletage cleavage lay down next to the skeleton, put her hand behind her head, and preened seductively like Lauren Bacall. Claver didn't respond, and Clark couldn't get his camera out fast enough to snap the picture. Religion and sex—that's what South America is about. But the women are on their own. They seemed to be free, able to choose. Jose, our guide, stopped trying to sell us emeralds to tell us a woman can go to a salon and get a pedicure, manicure, haircut, and an abortion, all for 16,000 pesos or about four dollars."

Clark shouted from the back of the room, "The guide's name was Luis, not Jose."

"Next, we tour the Palacio de la Inquisicion, where they have a rather interesting collection of torture instruments. Over 700 heretics (mostly women) died here after undergoing torture with the instruments on display. The chief inquisitor had been wont to worm secrets out of the accused and so used villainous machines for crushing thumbs and a devilish contrivance of iron, which enclosed a woman's head like a shell and crushed it slowly by means of a lever and a screw."

"Holy Mother, the One True Catholic and Apostolic Church, put women in this pleasant inquisition situation and pointed them to the Blessed Redeemer, Jesus, who was so gentle and so merciful toward all, and urged the barbarians to love him; and the priests did all they could to persuade them, the indigenous natives to love and honor him, first nipping their flesh with pincers, red hot ones, because they are most comfortable in cold weather; then by skinning them alive a little; and finally by roasting them in public at El Centro."

"But Clark and I didn't miss the sign on the wall:

Por favor no haga uso de los intrumentos de tortura—Gracias."

"Here we have the Tophet in Tunis where ancient Carthaginians sacrificed their children to Baal by passing the kids through fire, yes, burning their own live children to death, in hopes that Baal would help win the second Punic war. At the battle of Zama 202 BC, Baal didn't deliver, and Scipio, the Roman General, imposed harsh terms that Cartago had to accept. Burning your children is probably not a good idea. It spoils their weekend. In fact, sacrifices to gods probably never delivered anything of value to anyone. Recent studies show prayer is completely ineffective in helping people recover from surgery. One double-blind prospective study compared the prayed group with a sex- and age-matched control group. That study came out the wrong way. The prayed-for group did worse, much worse. Lesson: If I get sick, don't pray for me."

Hodge raised his hand again. "Sir, what does this travelogue have to do with the topics and contents of this course?"

"What's your name?" asked Meph-foe.

"Hodge, sir. With respect, I am just asking."

"Hodge, on April 15, 1755, Samuel Johnson published the most influential dictionary of the English language. Did you know that fact?"

"No, sir, I didn't."

"Do you know the name of Samuel Johnson's cat?"

"No, sir, I don't."

"You should look it up. If you do, you will find the cat's name had a very close resemblance to yours. Oh, hell, I'll save you the trouble. The cat's name was Hodge. And old Sam Johnson loved Hodge, no question. Even when there was a severe food shortage in London, Hodge got fed."

"You know, Hodge, you did the right thing. Asking questions, in many cases, gets to the truth. However, in many cases asking questions doesn't get anywhere. And you did the wrong thing, Hodge, asking a question, interrupting my class, and diverting the attention of many of your fellow students. That was a negative."

"In a certain sense, the travel pictures have little or nothing to do with this course, just part of coming to grips with what I believe is still one of the most unfinished business in human history— empowering women to be able to stand up for themselves. This is my course and my lecture. My aim is to show the yokels, like you and the other dumbbells in this class, a world they probably didn't even know existed. Foreign cultures and how they handle survival, people, and especially girls and women, are integral to our understanding of the human situation. This is especially true here in this hick town, Pasadena, in this shithole of a state, Texas. Most students here will never visit outside Texas, and they will be less for it because of the loss."

"I am trying to show them and you why they should travel and become acquainted with strange lands, strange cultures, and strange people. I am trying to show how women have been mistreated in various places and at various times and in various ways. Texas is, in many ways, the most worstest. Yes, the very worst in almost anything you can think of or name—child care, maternal care, gun deaths, infant mortality, and so forth. Texas has the highest rate of citizens who don't have health insurance, 17.3 %, according to U.S. census data. That's twice the national rate of 8.1% and three percentage points higher than the next worst state, Oklahoma."

"You name it. Texas is the pits. The one star in the Texas flag is what I would give this state: one star out of five, and if there were a lower rating, such as no stars, Texas would get it.

"Texas is number one nationwide in the number of banned books. Last year, Texas banned (according to PEN America, the American Association of Writers) 801 books in 22 school districts. The banned books deal with race, racism, abortion, and LGBTQ. Included in the ban is Toni Morrison's *The Bluest Eye*. That is not a nice way to treat a Nobel Laureate in Literature. Florida is second with 566 banned books, and Pennsylvania is third with 457. Texas School Boards believe in free speech and free information exchange, except when they don't. The banning of books in this state resembles Nazi attempts to control thought and has put a chill over the spirit of open inquiry. Better get your copies while you still can get them. One reviewer of the *Handmaiden's Tale* suggested you read that book before it is banned."

"Texas is also number one in incompetent government. Take, for example, the management of the 2021 freeze. According to the National Weather Service, the freeze lasted eight days, 23 hours, and 23 minutes. During that time, at least 702 people died directly or indirectly because of lack of heat. The damage exceeded that of Hurricane Harvey in 2017, making it the worst disaster in Texas history. I had nine blankets covering me and was still cold. Houston alone reported over 300 cases of carbon monoxide poisoning because people burned charcoal and other fuels in their unventilated homes, 4.5 million of which were without power. Total loss exceeded 195 billion dollars."

"Governor Abbott said the problem was caused by icing of wind turbines. That was bullshit—something done for effect without due regard as to whether it was true or not. Remember the definition of bullshit. It will be on the next test if I decide to give tests. Bullshit is something done for effect without due regard as to whether it is true or not. The other definition I want you to memorize is oppression. Oppression figures are large in the history of women, and it is important to know what exactly we are talking about when we use the word. Oppression is inequitable use of authority, law, or force to prevent others from being free or equal. Where was I? Oh, yeah, Abbott."

"Abbott even aired a video of a helicopter deicing a wind turbine. Subsequently, it was shown that the video was made in Sweden in 2015. Get it? There is no hesitancy to lie to the public to conceal incompetence and mismanagement. Then Abbott authorized release of one ton of benzene, a well-known cause of leukemia, two tons of sulfur dioxide, and 34 tons of carbon monoxide, setting a world record for air pollution."

"The number of cases of Acute Myeloblastic Leukemia here in Pasadena far exceeds the expected, and so does the incidence of pancreatic cancer. Texas city is the brain cancer center of America, probably because of pollution from the B.P. plant, but that's not all. Lawyers are now suing B.P. on behalf of many Texas City residents who got leukemia. The Busbee Lawyers have already collected millions for clients in Texas City who suffered leukemia. The causative agent in Texas City appears to be the aromatic hydrocarbon benzene, C_6H_6. Nasty stuff!"

"Back to the freeze."

"Senator Ted Cruz and family took off for Cancun. Cruz said it was a vacation planned long ago. More bullshit. The story changed when the emails from his wife surfaced, showing she wanted him and the family to scram. After that, Cruz said on TV that his daughters were to blame because they insisted he leave with them. More bullshit."

"Students, try to develop your own internal crap detector so you can immediately tell when these men are handing you bullshit."

Whew. Meph-foe was on his high horse, and taking notes fast enough was a problem. Some students had given up and were just listening, And some had fallen asleep. As for me, I wish I had learned shorthand."

"In 2011, federal authorities warned Texas that this would happen, but Texas remained off the two national power grids to keep out federal regulations."

"Here's my point: Who was in charge of this fiasco? Men or women?"

A beat while we tried to get the drift of all this, and for a beat, there was silence in the lecture hall. What was his point? What was Meph-foe driving at?"

Meph-foe repeated the question. "Men or women? Who was in charge of this fiasco? I am asking you directly. Who was in charge when Texas froze—men or women?"

This question was not rhetorical, so we all shouted out in unison, "Men!"

"Of course! Women would have been more caring and more protective of the public."

"Where was I?" Meph-foe scratched his head and looked around, and continued. "Oh, yes, travel."

"Travel broadens the mind. Broadens the mind. No doubt it does. Before I got sidetracked, that was my point, Hodge, before I got sidetracked. But this is a good time, as good a time as any, to segue into what I was really driving at. My real message."

"Books and reading."

"Travel broadens the mind. But reading does it better and faster and for less money and in less time. Books, good books, are the last refuge of the truth. THE TRUTH. Out there in this modern world, the level of misinformation and bullshit is so high I have to stand on my tiptoes to avoid suffocation. Truth has decayed. Decayed badly. The level of public discourse has reached the nadir, an all-time low. All-time low. Don't believe me? Just watch Fox News for five minutes. Complete and utter scallop slop."

"Pilate asked Jesus, 'What is truth?' The Bible doesn't say what Jesus answered, if indeed he did answer. Probably Jesus didn't answer. The question was too trivial. Jesus didn't say. So, I am going to tell you what is truth. Truth is what is as opposed to what is not. Truth is the real deal, the real situation, not a fake imagined load of crap and poppycock spread to make you believe things that are simply not so. Books, most of them, are still truthful, and they are so because they are made by scholars, men and women like myself who want you to know the truth. You shall know the truth, and the truth shall make you free. Some people thought that idea was so important they inscribed it on the floor at the entrance of Central Intelligence Agency headquarters in Langley, Virginia. The T-R-UTH (here Meph-foe spread the word out, elongating the pronunciation like those TV evangelists) shall make you free."

My seat was in the fifth row, in the center of that pretty big auditorium, now our lecture hall, and I was in the center of all this discourse. Nice place to see and hear everything. The one male in the class was seated in row four just under me, and I had a good view of his cute head with a real nice small bald spot right in the middle, a bald spot so cute I wanted to bend down and kiss it. If you had been paying attention, if you were still awake, you guessed he was my lust-worthy Hodge. Well, if you guessed right, good for you!

Hodge was wearing a bright red sweater full of holes from acid burns, sulfuric and nitric—this was the bad old days when chemistry students actually touched the chemicals. Now all that has changed, and men are not allowed to come near anything remotely dangerous. That is for their own protection and ours. Men just can't handle anything dangerous without causing trouble. Take away the means, and you prevent the ends. That's how we women ended the mass shooting in America. Just take away the guns, and nobody can shoot nobody.

Back to Hodge.

Then and there, I fell in love with him. He looked like he needed someone to take care of him, and that was going to be me. It was love at first sight. When two hesitate, the love is slight. Whoever loved who loved not at first sight. Shakespeare and, as usual ,true, true, true.

Just before the bell, Meph-foe curled his lip in a strange, almost angry way, and a tremor came into his voice. Suddenly in the lecture hall, not even a breath was heard. He looked angry, almost like he wanted to kill someone.

"I have never seen anything so bad as this country run by men. They must be removed from power, and a kinder, gentler, more simpatico rule imposed.

"Men no longer should be in charge of anything. Women should call the shots. In my next lecture, I will prove that men have been extremely bad for civilization, and I will prove beyond a reasonable doubt by evidence that is relevant and sufficient that men are not fit to govern and should be removed from power.

I was stunned. Others were too. Gasps and sighs arose and then died down. And then bursts of hoots and whistles and loud applause and stamping of feet in rhythm and almost all together in a kind of very unladylike entrainment.

The din dimmed down, and the group started to pack up. I slowly closed my notebook and dropped the pen into my purse. Wow! What a lecture.

There, sitting on the edge of the chair and holding my breath. I shook my head yes, yes, yes. This was the right course and the right teacher for me. He was verbose, but for good reasons.

Hodge emitted a short sigh and fell back limply. He was utterly exhausted, yet exhilarated too.

A great man had spoken the invincible truth universally acknowledged that we all wanted to hear. A truly great man. I am in the presence of a truly great man. A great teacher and a great professor. How would I ever talk to him? What would I say? I would love a conversation. But about what? For what do I know? I decided to go straight to the library and read for the rest of the afternoon. Then I remembered during break, I had promised Hodge I would go with him for coffee. Darn Hodge, anyway. Darn it! Something always stops me from being the scholar I should be. I hope Hodge doesn't expect much on our first date. Usually, I don't go to bed on the first date. Usually don't means sometimes do.

Let's see.

CHAPTER THREE

AMONTILLADO FROM JEREZ, SPAIN

"A wrong is unredressed when retribution overtakes its redresser."

—Edgar Allen Poe

So, I suppose y'all out there in reader land out of prurient interest want to know what happened on our first date. That, I suppose, is normal, and I urge you to pause now and think about this and decide what you think happened and what you think should happen. Later check your ideas to see how right and how wrong you were. The title of this chapter might or might not give you a clue. Who knows? What happens on a first date is contingent, like most things in life. Usually, I don't go to bed on the first date, but *"usually don't"* means I sometimes do, especially if someone gives me a good reason. Let's see what happened:

Hodge and I had coffee in the cafeteria, a dull yellow space crowded with youthful energy and enthusiasm and loud choruses of male and female voices. The coffee, as any of you who have been to college expected, looked, smelled, and tasted like dishwater. If it had any caffeine in it, it was of no effect like the neutrinos from outer space that pass through us every second, effecting no effect, no nothing.

Hodge had his coffee black, and mine was cream and sugar. Just after we sat down in a quiet corner, Lorrie joined us with interesting news.

Lorrie: "Jesus, I just had an experience right out of the twilight zone. It wasn't with Rod Serling. It was with Meph-foe."

"After class, Clark came down the hall and tapped me on the shoulder. He said, "Professor Mephistopheles wants to see you in his office.""

"What? The course just started. What could he possibly want? I didn't do nothing. Are you sure he wants me?"

Clark nodded, made a sour face like a child rejecting a breast, shrugged his shoulders, and said, "He didn't say. But he wants you now. Yes, you."

Hodge sat up straight, "Highly irregular. I hope you didn't go, and if you did—on guard."

Lorrie: "Meph-foe, his office was small, dark, and dusty. Kind of claustrophobic. Books lined the walls from floor to ceiling, except for a small window that overlooks the parking lot and a door on the north side that led to another room. Meph-foe's desk, cluttered with papers, was large and old-fashioned with that cover that rotates and folds down. There's a dark blue couch by the south wall, a small table in the center of the room on which was a bottle of sherry."

Mephistopheles: "Ah, Lorrie. Many thanks for coming. I like to get to know my students and make them feel at home and comfortable. You are looking great. Care for a drop of sherry? I like to take a drop in the afternoons. It's much better than tea. Some people prefer tea. Not me. Too much trouble. Sherry for me. I like the way it looks—light brown. I like the way it smells—herbal. I like the way it tastes—slightly nutty, complex, and intriguing. I like the way it makes me feel—happy and relaxed. This one is from Jerez,

Spain, fortified to 17.5%, a gift from the poet laureate Professor Loccul. It is not a good sherry. It is a great sherry. It's Almacenista Amontillado de Sanlucar."

Lorrie: "What the hell could I do? He had already poured the glass and handed it to me before I could say a word. He was right; it was delicious, as he said. But while I was admiring the clear golden-brown color of the cooling drink (how had he chilled it? There must be a refrig in the adjacent room), Meph-foe got in back of me, slipped his arm around my neck and pawed with his right hand down toward my tit. He was prepared like a boy scout. I said, "Amontillado—I've heard that before."

Mephistopheles whispering in my right ear: "No doubt. It figures in a very famous 1846 short story by Edgar Allen Poe, *The Cask of Amontillado*. Let's see if I can quote the beginning: 'The thousand injuries of Fortinato I had borne as best I could, but when he ventured upon insult, I vowed revenge.'"

Crash! Bam!

"Meph-foe had pinched my nipple, not hard but enough to scare me, and I had dropped the beautiful Longchamp crystal glass by Eclat, the kind my mom collects and displays in a glass cabinet. Sherry aroma filled the room, and shards of glass spread out on the brown oak floor. 'Ugh! I'm so sorry. I am so sorry!'"

"No problem, Lorrie. Clark will clear the mess. Would you like another?

"No thanks. I have to leave."

"Lorrie, can we speak frankly?"

"Yes. I have to leave. If you touch me again, I'll scream, and you can bet I'll file a complaint."

"Lorrie, some men like myself have a gigantic urge that must be satisfied. We are suffering, suffering greatly. Women like you can help stop our suffering. You can help us. You have a moral obligation. Please help."

"No. The answer is no."

"Lorrie, girls who give are girls who get. I'm sure you have heard that before. It's true. And girls who do not give are girls who don't get. Your female form attracts me with an undeniable attraction. Beauty is a great calling card in this wide world. You should use it to further your interests. Your body is not something you just carry around. Make it work for you."

"The answer is no."

"Please, Lorrie. Be reasonable. If you are worried about pregnancy, forget it. I shoot blanks."

"No!"

"Ugh! Miss, I am disappointed with your attitude and would find myself in the position of not giving you any grade but a C-. Do you get my drift?"

"Yes and no. You, professor, will actually give me an A. And I will tell you why."

"You're dreaming. No cooperation means C- not A."

"Nope. An A."

"At this point, I pulled out my iPhone and pushed it into his fat face. See this! I recorded you and every goddamn thing you said."

"That's illegal, Lorrie. Completely illegal. I can sue, or I think I can."

"So what! Sue away. When they hear this shit, you will be in hot water. No, change that. You will be in boiling hot water and cooked. Meanwhile, fuck off!"

"And then I gave him the finger and said, 'Up yours, professor. Up yours!'"

"OK. You win, Lorrie. Let's make a deal. You be nice to me, and I will be nice to you. As all the students know, grades are on the curve: ten percent A, twenty percent B, and the rest C and a few D and F and incomplete as I see fit. You will get the one A+ in the class. Please erase the recording. OK?"

"A is good enough for me. I don't need an A+. No harm will come to you from the recording if you play ball. Goodbye and good luck, professor."

"Please, Lorrie. Be nice. What?"

"You still don't get it! You jerk. Fuck you." Again the finger jerking up and down. "'Fuck off,' I screamed. 'Fuck off!'"

Lorrie smiled and said, "Pretty cool, right? I walked. I am getting an A, and I didn't even have to put out."

Me (Lollipop): "Disgraceful. A messy, human interaction between teacher and student. Not new and not nice, but probably common. His approach was wrong. But, Lorrie, your conduct was reprehensible. Recording a private chat is not nice. And you were impolite in the extreme. This man is on our side. I would have considered it an honor and a privilege to get laid by him. A great honor. For he is a great man, a very great man. He was suffering, and you didn't lift a finger to help. Shame, shame on you."

"Andzelika, you're wrong."

Me: "Call me Lollipop."

"It's Polish, right? Andzelika. Does it mean anything?"

"Messenger of God. My last name is just as bad: Dziedzic, meaning landowner."

"OK, Lollipoop."

"Lollipop! Not Lollipoop. Don't make fun of my name. It's Lollipop. Like candy, candy on a stick."

"OK. You do things your way, and I will do things my way. For your info, I didn't record anything. I don't even know how to do it. But he thinks I did, which is just as good and will have the same effect. I got an A, and I didn't even have to hit the blue couch, take a test, or write a term paper or book review. You can major in couch if you wish. That's your business. As for me, no way. Besides, I like girls. I prefer to scissor and not get plugged. Men, in general, are low down, dirty, and deceitful."

Me: "What do you think, Hodge?"

Hodge: "Me? It is not my job to think or reason why, but to do and die," Hodge smiled, thinking he was being clever by misreciting lines from *The Charge of the Light Brigade* by Alfred, Lord Tennyson about the ill-advised charge and subsequent slaughter of British troops at the battle of Balaclava in the Crimean War. "Both of you have intelligent points of view. But, if I had to take sides, I would side with you, Lollrie,"

"I'm Lorrie."

"Lorrie, you followed your bliss and lit your star. Good for you. Lollipop, you sound man-struck, penis-struck. Meph-foe is a Professor. Meph-foe is right out of central casting—urbane, articulate, humorous, witty, gracious, a slick magazine hero, and well dressed in a pin-striped charcoal Brooks Brothers three-piece suit, the kind that went out of fashion decades ago. But he is also a satyr.

"His knowledge is vast and deep, and one wondered why he was teaching at a Junior College and not at Columbia or Harvard or Brown or some other Ivy League University. Probably he had gotten into trouble. Probably something sexual, I would say. He looked the type. It's in the eyes and in the wan wistful smile. I've been around. I can spot them a mile away. Men on the make.

"Meph-foe has enchanting anecdotes up his sleeve for every topic and every question and occasion. He could explain anything and everything with facts and details in the charming turn of a phase and a certain originality that was his hallmark. With his white mustache, white beard, and silver hair (why pretend you are not old?), all us students find him charming and distinguished. That, of course, was the desired effect—what he was looking for, working for.

Me: OK, I apologize. Dear reader, that's not what Hodge said. I just, more or less, copied that stuff from what I wrote previously. That's what I would have liked him to say. What would have put us on the same page with concordance. What Hodge said was different and somewhat annoying.

Hodge: "Prof is full of himself. Too full. He likes facts and details. That's clear, so I, for one, will be including lots of facts and details on the tests and papers. Professor cherry-picks the facts to suit his convenience, and he lacks nuance. That is a bad attitude for a scientist or a scholar but is the usual attitude of a politician and a used car salesman. He claims to favor the truth and yet twists and bends the facts for his convenience and to persuade us he is right. This country has problems, lots of them, but it seems unjust to ignore the fact that we are free, prosperous, and one of the world's greatest economic, political, and military powers. That fact, our arrival at this point in history is mainly due to the guidance and leadership of great men like George Washington, FDR, and Obama.

"My prediction is that prof will be citing all the bad men in history, like Stalin, Hitler, Putin, and Mussolini, to make it look like men and men alone are responsible for the current problems and the big mess.

"Prof's behavior toward you, Lorrie, or Lotte, whatever, is probably more normal and typical of male teachers and men in power all across the land. Trump is probably more mainstream among American men than is generally acknowledged. He said he could grab a pussy, and most women wouldn't mind. There was pay-off hush money to some porn star, and so forth. This behavior in a man who nevertheless was elected president! It isn't right, and I don't condone it. The power relations are wrong. True love and good sex, in my view, can and should only occur between equals. Well, anyway, that's my two cents. I'll see you all in class Wednesday. Meanwhile, I'm going to shoot pool with Clark."

CHAPTER FOUR

LECTURE TWO

"Ye shall know them by their fruits. Do men gather grapes of thorns or figs of thistles? Even so, every good tree bringeth forth good fruit, but a corrupt tree bringeth forth evil fruit."

—Mathew 7: 16, 17

Ok, I was disappointed with Hodge and our first date. And I bet you were too. There was lots of discussion. That was good, but he didn't seem one bit interested in me. And the most unkind cut of all was he didn't even suggest we go back to his place if he had one or his dorm room if he had one. Instead, he took off with Clark to shoot pool.

Clark will probably take Hodge to the cleaners. Serves him right. Another negative: Hodge had trouble keeping his eyes off of Lorrie's rack. She is stacked. Men just can't keep their eyes off big tits. Life can be cruel. Her boobs are hall-of-fame perfect. It was nice of her to admit she likes girls. That helped level the playing field. She must be a real lesbo since she knew about scissoring. I knew about it from Cherry Bomb, my friend from the Psych Ward Sirens of Houston's Roller Derby. Cherry Bomb and Jekyll and Heidi and Merciless Mary are an item, a folie a trois (Jekyll and Heidi is one person. That's her Roller Derby name.). They do a great whip it and plow together. And, according to Cherry Bomb, they do great scissoring. As for me, I have not had the privilege and probably won't ever. Some, like me, are just too hetero. How about you?

* * * * *

Meph-foe entered stage right. Put his big black book of lecture notes on the podium, opened to a page, licked his lips, frowned, and then closed the book. He decided to wing it, give us something extemporaneous, off the cuff, and discursive as was his wont and style. Looking over the group, he smiled and waved at Lorrie. God, he must be a psychopath after what happened. Lorrie didn't wave back.

"Welcome back. Glad to see so many of you. Clark takes attendance, but that is just for my interest and curiosity. It will have nothing to do with your grade. Attendance is not required. You are adults, and you need to decide for yourselves whether to attend class or do something better like sleep. Grades are mainly based on your papers. Which reminds me, interesting word, "reminds," meaning brings back into the mind, reminds me I want each of you to write a two-page paper, typed double spaced, and put it in the lock box in front of my office by 6 o'clock Friday. Make sure it is only two pages. I won't read beyond two pages. Select any topic related to the course. I read and grade all the papers myself and will have them all back to you by next week. The good ones I copy and keep in my file for future reference. Believe it or not, I love reading student papers. It tells me a lot about what the youth is thinking. You are the future, and I respect you for that fact."

"And like most humans, I would like some insights about the future, insights that might inform me about investment opportunities or insights that might make me want to hang myself. Most student papers will be trash band not worthy of the gentleman C grade they will receive, but among the trash, there will be many gems, many gems. Here's a hint of what I expect: Make it interesting and make it real using real facts and details. And don't copy anything from the internet. I can spot that crap right away, and you will get a big fat F for the effort."

"In the last lecture, which by the way, was the first lecture, interesting turn of phrase—the last was the first; therefore, the word last is ambiguous. In the last lecture, I tried to make a few points, among which were the ideas that travel and reading confer personal benefits. The most important part of that lecture, in my view, was the definition of bullshit, which I asked you all to memorize. Bullshit is something or anything done for effect without due regard as to whether it is true or not. Equipped with the definition, you will be better able to identify bullshit in its many forms. Simply apply the definition as a criterion."

"For example: take the slogan "Make America Great Again" and unpack it. Is it bullshit or not? Well, let's see. If the person saying that slogan believes it, he is stating as a fact that America is not great at present but was great at some time in the past, and he is urging his base or whoever will listen to believe him. Consider this: Is America great at present or not? What is the truth? What is the reality? Considering that America is the great economic, political, social, and military power it is, we must conclude that MAGA is bullshit—something done for effect without due regard as to whether it is true or not. As the slogan is bullshit, obviously done for effect, we conclude that the person saying it is a bullshitter and not to be trusted. Get it? Think of this: Either he believes it, or he doesn't. Which is worse? If he doesn't believe it, he is still a bullshitter and also a scallywag, a mountebank, a liar, a deceiver, and in my view, a public menace."

"We also learned in our first lecture that theocracies in Mayan and Aztec civilizations murdered humans for rather dubious reasons to appease the gods. In subsequent lectures, we will discuss the defect in the human brain called the reification phenomena, in which people think, because they were able to think about something, that it actually was real. Because some people can think a pure spirit can, by saying a few words create the entire universe, they tend to think that spirit is real when in reality is just an idea in their head."

"Blasphemy!" The old woman screamed from the back of the room. At the time, I didn't know her name. Meph-foe subsequently told us her name was Gertrude Jones, or was it Gertrude Smith? I forget. No matter. Miss Jones or Smith continued, "Blasphemy! I can tell by the way you talk you don't believe in God."

"I beg your pardon, madam, I am God, and Jesus Christ is my chauffeur waiting downstairs for me in the limo."

Wow! Meph-foe's reply was a stinger. That will teach her. No answer to that. Gertrude left and probably would drop the course. Will she cause trouble? Will she get her tuition back? I say yes to both those questions, but we'll see. Students these days are set to complain about anything and any little thing. That's what Deans are for. The Deans are the flack takers. The students Mau-Mau, the flack takers.

Meph-foe continues as if nothing special has happened. "You also were told in that first lecture that there exists in Patagonia a special male frog named after Darwin who carries tadpoles in its vocal sac until they are ready to face the world. At the next dinner party, try to work that fact into the conversation, and you will look very smart. By the way, raise your hand if you looked up Patagonia."

No hands.

"When you hear something you don't know about or are not sure you know about, write it down and look it up. If you hear a word you don't know, write it down and look it up. That is the way to expand your knowledge and eventually look like me—ten times smarter. Notice I said *look* ten times smarter, not be ten times smarter. I am actually a very dumb person, but I know how to look smart."

"Patagonia (pronounced "pata yonja" in Spanish), is a region at the southern end of South America governed by Argentina and Chile. The region comprises the southern end of the Andes mountains with lakes, fjords, rainforests in the west, and deserts and steppes in the east. Humbert, in that very famous novel which I am sure most of you haven't read but may have heard of—*Lolita*—that's what I am talking about. Humbert, the protagonist, wants to call Pat in Patagonia. So, by that clang association, we learn that H.H. is not entirely right in the head."

"riverrun, past Eve and Adam's, from swerve of shore to bend of bay, brings us by a commodious vicus of recirculation back to today's lecture, which, unlike ancient Gaul, consists of only two parts. Part one before the break and part two after."

"Let me start with an introduction to analogy. Analogy is a way of comparing things so that we can uncover properties that they have in common and discover what they don't. Some analogies lead to tremendous insights, and others lead nowhere because every analogy must break down because the two items, although they may be similar, will have some different properties as they are, by definition, different. If they were not different in some way, they would be the same and, therefore, not subject to analogy. Students understand this kind of abstraction if it is illustrated with an example, for instance:"

"Suppose you hire a contractor to build a house. Subsequently, you discover the electric system is defective, the water pipes leak, the slab is cracked, and part of the roof blew away in a storm. Who will you blame? The postman? Your wife? The local doctor? The third-grade school teacher? President Biden? Who?"

"Hodge. Who is to blame?"

Poor Hodge. He had dozed off, and that's why Meph-foe called on him.

"What's up?" asked Hodge, still dazed by sleep.

"Hodge, try to pay attention. I know it is difficult. You were sleeping in class. I asked who would you blame for the poor construction?"

"What construction?"

"Right, Hodge. You don't know. That is the only reasonable answer for you to give because you don't know. And, class, this is an excellent example of what happens if you are not paying attention to what is happening. Neglect of the situation, and you are lost. What's the lesson? The lesson is PAY ATTENTION."

"Who knows the answer? Yes, you in row five. Sorry I don't know your name."

"Andzelika Dziedzic, sir."

"Ye gods, what a terrible name. Why not change it so your friends can say it, right? Well, your answer, please, miss whatever."

"Obviously, there is enough blame to go around, The electrician who did a poor job, the plumber ditto, the foundation man, and so forth. But in general, the blame should fall on the person in charge, and that would be the contractor."

"That's right. So true. The blame must be assigned to the person or persons in charge. Keep that in mind when we review a host of contemporary problems. Modern America has no lack of problems. Some problems, we can tell right away who is to blame. Mass shooting—was there ever a mass shooting not done by a man? How about serial killers? Can you name any serial killers who are women? What about the large collection of minatory men who have brought wars of terrible suffering on humanity—Hitler, Stalin, and Putin, to name a few? Were any of these gangster leaders women? Of course not. Which gender provides the most suicide bombers? Is there any crime that men don't commit? Robbery, embezzlement, theft, murder… the deadly sins. Is there a vice for which they don't have a license or claim a license? What gender is more likely to press the button to cause a thermonuclear war?"

He paused so we could let all that sink in. Then Meph-foe carried on.

"And now, out of concern for the elimination of gun violence in America, let's look at some facts. Robert Frost said the fact was the sweetest thing that nature knows. And he was right. Facts are the keys to a persuasive argument. Facts not only tell us the problem exists, but they tell the dimension of the problem so we can estimate how much energy, time, and money and especially public knowledge will be needed to solve the problem."

There followed a comprehensive discussion of gun violence in America and the clear conclusion that men are to blame. Meph-foe gave it for his opinion that our male leaders are catering to and currying favor from a minority of men who like guns and won't tolerate much in the way of gun control. My notes summarize what Meph-foe said, and I briefly list some of the highlighted items for those of you who might be interested. Not interested? Shame on you. This is a national problem. How would you like to have your children killed in school? How would you have liked to be killed in a July parade, a church meeting, or a rock concert in Las Vegas, or at the supermarket when you are trying to buy some peppers or bananas?

The dead are not just data points. They were husbands, wives, teachers, grandparents, friends, relatives, real people whose lives were cut short. Real people like you whose lives were cut short. See how I learned to repeat just like Meph-foe. Repeat for emphasis. That's the ticket.

When we women took over, all weapons were taken from some men. Actually, after we took over, most men didn't want to have anything to do with weapons. Guns, they felt, were the pathos of a civilization now vanished. Men are just too dangerous and too stupid to be trusted with any weapon whatsoever. And the results speak for themselves. No guns meant no gun deaths. It was that simple, and only we women could have done it.

Meph-foe: "Kiddies, guns are bad. Consider the following facts and draw your conclusions about who is to blame."

Meph-foe got choked up when he came to the Uvalde massacre at the Robb Elementary School. He said he was thinking of Angeli Rose Gomez, a farm worker who had two children trapped inside while 376 law enforcement officers were present and doing nothing to bring down the active gunman. Mrs. Gomez broke loose from police restraint, jumped a fence, and rescued her kids and their classmates herself.

Meph-foe's voice faltered. He was crying. Yes, actually crying. And he had to stop. God, I hate to see grown men cry. He blew his nose, wiped his eyes but still couldn't stop. He sat on a chair next to Clark, who patted him on the shoulder. Meph-foe leaned forward with his hands on both knees. Now, this looked like a hyperventilation attack. Clark gave some yellow drink and, I think, a white pill. When the attack was over, Meph-foe started again:

"Sorry. I got carried away thinking of all the dead boys and girls and the teachers and the stupid police who were afraid of their shadows. Whew! What a mess. My heart was in the coffins there with them, and I had to wait for it to return to me."

"Let's talk about 19 days in America! Over the last 19 days, a vast number of other Americans, including a one-year-old in Maine and a 94-year-old in Missouri, were killed by firearms. In that 19-day period, 2,348 people fell prey to our country's relentless and monstrous public health crisis. Every gun death is preventable."

"The mass shootings in Buffalo, New York, Laguna Woods, California, Uvalde, Texas, and Tulsa, Oklahoma, are heart-wrenching tragedies. For many of us, it is almost impossible to look upon the faces of the victims and the grief of their families. After all, we, too, are parents or will be, and we, too, were children, and we know people who are spouses, uncles, aunts, friends, and cousins. We are all the same species, and in my view, one of our responsibilities is to prevent these terrible things from happening. Yes, it is we who must play a role in stopping the epidemic of gun violence that is shaking our country. We must become effective agents of prevention."

"The latest episodes of mass murder bring to mind the many similar shootings we have witnessed during the past few years. Yet mass shootings represent only one part of the problem of gun violence in America."

"According to the Centers for Disease Control and Prevention, there were 45,222 firearm-related deaths from homicide, suicide, unintentional injuries, and police-involved shootings in the United States in 2020, the most recent year for which data are available. That means in a 19-day period in America (the time between the massacres in a Buffalo grocery store and a Tulsa medical center), gun violence killed 2,348 people."

"Sad to say, gun violence is now the leading cause of death among U.S. children and adolescents. Get that? The leading cause of death among children and adolescents. Many more people—often adolescents and young adults—sustain nonfatal firearm-related injuries, which can leave them with permanent disabilities and mental anguish. These survivors, many of them, become life-long dependents on the public welfare."

"And think of this: the ripple effect of a gunshot reaches far beyond those struck by a bullet, devastating families and neighborhoods and disproportionately affecting communities of color. Grandparents—devastated!"

Meph-foe paused. He was choked up again. Jesus, he's a mess, a pitiable mess. He let out a large hunk of breath, shrugged his shoulders, and continued.

"In one sense, these killings are senseless, but tragically, they do make sense: we are seeing exactly the results the system is designed to achieve. We know that most countries have vastly lower rates of firearm violence and deaths. And yet we in the United States choose to give ready access to weapons of war to people who will use them to hurt themselves and destroy others. Why?"

Meph-foe got choked up again. He looked out at us with a strange inquiry face, a sad face, and then he sobbed and started to cry.

"Sorry. I can't continue. Too shook up. Too dizzy. Got a bad pain in the pit of my stomach. I hope I'm not having a heart attack or appendicitis or something. Let's take a break. Come back in 15 minutes. I may be in shape to continue, and I may not be in shape. Time will tell. We are all travelers in time, the semi-elastic substance that is, according to Einstein, the same material thing as space though measured differently."

Break:

I went to the bathroom, brushed my hair, adjusted my makeup, applied some *Intimate* by Revlon, my perfume, and made a beeline for Hodge. He was outside in the sweltering Texas heat smoking a cigarette (Marlboro Ultra Lite 0.8 mg tar and 0.6 mg nicotine by FTC method).

Hodge was standing under a pin oak tree 50 feet, the required distance from the entrance. That's another thing we women did when we took over. No more smoking for men and no drinking alcohol or coffee. We needed healthy X chromosome-carrying sperms to remake human society into one sex and one sex only—namely, all female. Besides, giving up the smokes was good not only for sperm health but for male health in general, although the men didn't see it that way when push came to shove.

"Hodge, you shouldn't smoke. It might stunt your growth. Er, can I have a drag?"

"Yes, you can. But nope. You may not. It might stunt your growth. Or give you cancer, heart disease, and any other goddamn thing they can think of. Oh, hell, here."

I inhaled deep and long. Wow, when the nicotine hit the blood, my fingers and toes tingled, and a serene calm came over my brain. Nicotine is the solace of a troubled world, or at least it was until we took over. People get addicted to nicotine because it is addicting.

I decided to show off for Hodge, show him how cool I am, so I took a big puff and blew a smoke ring.

A smoke ring: the blue-white circle rose from boiling within its own form, hovered for an instant, then melted into an entropic weaving strand. It was beautiful, a thing of beauty, but like any beauty, it faded and then disappeared.

Hodge gave a sideward glance, smiled, and made the give-me sign with his right hand. There was a pause, a beat. He was thinking, thinking of something. Staring at me. And thinking. About what?

"Hodge, what do you make of Meph-foe?"

"He's OK, I guess. Likes to show off. Knows lots. A real smarty pants. He's in the right profession. Good teacher. I like the way he works in famous quotes to suit himself. Did you get the one from *The Tragedy of Julius Caesar*? 'My heart is in the coffin there with Caesar, and I must pause till it come back to me.' Only with Meph-foe, with him, it was the boys and girls and three teachers from Uvalde in the coffins. Most students, I bet, missed the reference to the beginning of James Joyce's *Finnegans Wake*—riverrun, swerve of shore. Something like that he used to return to the topic under discussion, which was men and the violence men cause. You doing anything tonight?"

"Working in the library on the paper Meph-foe assigned. Why?"

"I was thinking about a date. How about a date?"

"Nope. I am working on the paper. How about Friday after the papers are turned in? We can relax and unwind."

"OK. Friday after we turn in the papers. Dinner and a date? What say?

"Sure. Meet at the box just before sex."—I blushed at the Freudian slip. "Meet at the box just before SIX. I'll bring a copy of my paper so I can read it to you. How about you do the same?"

"Meet at six. Good. But I don't know about reading my paper. I don't even know what I am going to write. Do you?"

"Nope. But I know it will be good. I have an A.B. and a masters from Yale in English lit. and creative writing. I am as skilled at writing as I am making smoke rings."

"Holy cow! What the hell are you doing here taking a course in this rinky-dink Junior college?"

"Top secret. I may tell, and I may not tell as I see fit, and Hodge, you should know that I usually don't go to bed on the first date."

"Nor do I. And you should know I used to have a sexual thought every 27 seconds. Now it's more like every two minutes. You're Lollipop, right."

"Gosh! You remembered my name?"

"I've been around, same as you. I was at the cafeteria, remember? I left you, girls, to play pool. By the way, Meph-foe has at least one gigantic fan, a man who not only loves him but also worships him.

Clark! I learned that fact while playing billiards. Clark has been around. Semi-professional, I would say. He took me for 52 bucks, fair and square. And I learned things like how to use the rosin on the cue to put the desired spin on the ball and how to take advantage of the net weave on the green glaze to pocket. But, of course, I won't play again with him. I'm not stupid."

* * * * *

Back to class:

"Welcome back. I am much better after a little refreshment and rest, and I hope you all feel the same. In this session, I want to discuss the recent decisions of the United States Supreme Court. The format for the discussion will resemble that used by Saint Thomas Aquinas in his book Summa Theologica. This was one of the earliest forms of reasoned discourse and the kind of thing our country and the world would greatly benefit from following."

"We must start with some definitions. Remember, if you are talking about something and you don't know the definition of what you are talking about, then you, quite literally, actually do not know what you are talking about. It's a fault common in current political discourse and something we must avoid. We start with something simple—the definition of a statement."

"A statement is a sentence that makes a definite claim. For example: If I say, "It is raining," that is a statement because it is a sentence and makes a definite claim. The claim is that it is raining. Also understood are the existential claims attached to each statement. In this case, it is asserted that rain exists and that something, namely, *IT* (atmospheric conditions where the temperature drops below the dew point), is making it rain. Get it? If you don't get it, reread your notes several times until it sinks in. And memorize the definition."

"A statement at a given time in a given place is always true or false. If it is raining, then the statement is true, and if it is not raining, the statement is false. The existential claims of a statement can be tricky so pay careful attention to them. For example, "God is just" is a statement that also claims God exists and just exists. That statement caused lots of trouble for Catholic logicians because if God is just, then God is bound by an extra deific standard and therefore can't be all-powerful. If God is not all-powerful, then he can't be God. Get it?"

"Medieval philosophers concluded that it is not possible for God to be God and just at the same time, and as that can't be true, the statement must be false, and God is not just. No bull. That is what they reasoned, and they came up with the idea that although God is not just, He is justice itself. Here's another statement to consider. See if you can unpack it as homework by discovering the major claim, the existential claim, and the subaltern claims:"

"We are the Master Race."

—Adolph Hitler

"An argument is a group of statements, and a case is a collection of arguments. Knowing those definitions, let's proceed with our Thomistic analysis of the United States Supreme Court, something I have recently started calling the Extreme Court. This analysis is important because it shows how the radical right is trying to take over. The actual format is argument followed by objection, just like the many arguments and objections that appear in the summa."

Meph-foe paused and stepped in front of the podium to get closer to us. He held his hands on high as a sign of disgust.

"Kiddies, It was a very bad week in June, portending many bad weeks to come. Within the space of seven days, the conservative supermajority on the US Supreme Court issued three rulings that revoked a fundamental right from half of the population and decimated the wall of separation between church and state. In my view, the Supreme Court used constitutional law as a subterfuge to impose religious dogma on the entire nation. See if you agree."

"Argument: Carson v. Makin (June 21): The court ruled Maine's system of funding public education, in which the state pays for children to attend private schools in rural areas without a public school, violated the Free Exercise Clause of the First Amendment by excluding explicitly religious schools."

"Objection 1.: It would seem that now taxpayers in Maine, whether they are atheist, agnostic, Deist, Muslim, Jewish, Buddhist, Hindu, Aztec, Satanist, or any other religious faith, will now be forced to pay for children to be indoctrinated with religious viewpoints they reject and may even find abhorrent. Yes, soon, taxpayers will be forced to pay for schools that have openly stated they believe evolution and the teaching of it is a Satanic plot and that the earth is only 6,000 years old. Taxpayers will now be forced to support religious schools that have openly stated boys and girls will be separated and given separate and different curricula."

"Objection 2. It would seem anti-democratic for the officials of these schools to openly teach prejudice against gays and lesbians and transgender students, as they said they would."

"Objection 3. It would seem religious leaders are exploiting the taxpayers, for they have found many ways to pick taxpayer pockets, including massive tax exemptions on property and salaries. Now the Extreme Court has given still another way, having ruled Maine is powerless to regulate its own affairs to prevent it. This is even more egregious considering that one-third of the population list themselves as NONES, meaning they have no religious affiliation."

"Hodge, no need to raise your hand if you need to go to the bathroom. Just get up and go."

"I don't need to go. I have a question."

"Hodge, I thought I made it crystal clear I don't want my lectures interrupted. Questions disturb my train of thought and are discourteous to the other students here who want to hear me and learn from me and not hear or learn from you."

"OK, I don't have a question. I have a comment."

"Class, did you see what Hodge just did? He avoided the question rule by changing to a comment. Very interesting, Hodge, a common trick. But this does give me the opportunity to explain the art of argument. First, there is the conjecture and then the answer. For instance, I say you stole my car. That's the conjecture. An answer might be a denial, namely: No, I didn't. Thus, the point of contention would be established and evidence presented to decide the truth. The next possible answer is usually a definition change, which indirectly affirms the conjecture, at least in part. That goes like this: You stole my car. Answer: No, I didn't. I just borrowed it without your permission."

"Get it? The respondent admits the car was taken but changes the definition of the issue from a steal to a borrow. The third item in traditional argument is a value statement. That goes like this: You stole my car. Answer: Yes, I took it, and it is a good thing I did. A man fell in front of your home and broke his hip. I took him to the hospital in your car. If I had not, the lawsuit against you might have been much worse."

"In the usual classical form of argument, the last item is a venue argument. That goes like this: You stole my car. Answer: This is not the time or place to discuss this issue. We'll settle this in court. And that is why the school issue ended up in the Supreme Court to settle the dispute."

"Hodge has already changed the argument by changing the definition, and I expect if he is following classical rhetoric, he will make some sort of value claim for his interruption."

Hodge stood and turned his back on Meph-foe and spoke to us directly: "Public discourse these days is full of changes of frame and definition to appeal to larger audiences. Most people are not pro-abortion. They are pro-choice. Most people are not anti-abortion. They are pro-life. What I did was a trick to get to say what I feel needs to be said and understood."

"OK, Hodge, you admit you probably had a question, but when reminded about the rule of no questions in class, the question morphed into a comment. Isn't that right, Hodge?"

Hodge turned to face Meph-foe. "Yes, sir! Exactly right. Any question can be turned into a comment and vice versa. What I need to say was that, in my view, you overemphasized the importance and influence of the Supreme Court's decision, and you tried to diminish our respect for the court by calling the Supreme Court the Extreme Court. Political hysteria and overreaction are serious negative aspects of American political discourse. How many religious nut cases can there be in Maine, and how many schools in rural areas are we talking about? It's hard for me to believe people still don't believe in evolution. It is even harder for me to believe there are some who think the earth is only 6,000 years old. But my complaint goes further. You, sir, are significantly out of step with modern thinking about the nature of teaching and learning. There are known methods of teaching that allow more people of different backgrounds to master material through discussions and questions, and problem-solving. Consider using active learning methods that engage students as opposed to their passively taking in information from a dull and often boring lecture."

Wow! Hodge has guts. No question about it. It's interesting that in a class of 200, the only troublemaker is the man. The rest of us women are too busy scribbling down Meph-foe's immortal words. This is a lesson for us women on how to take over. We have to be more assertive, less passive, and more bitchy, if you will. To get control of society, we have to copy the methods men use, methods they seem to know naturally and automatically. Copy the masters. That's key. Copy the master to become masters. In my notebook, I wrote a note to myself: *Lollipop, develop female temerity. Work on it and do it soon.*

"Have you finished, Hodge?" asked Meph-foe with a kind of condescending tone and an enigmatic smile. His face looked happy, too happy. Meph-foe has something up his sleeve.

"Not quite. I wanted to make the point about taxes. Considering the number of taxpayers in Maine and the minute effect the addition of one or a few religious schools would have on what each individual taxpayer would pay, the issue is too trivial to merit attention or discussion. The state of Maine probably spent more money on legal fees than they will ever spend for these religious schools."

"OK, Hodge, I have a question for you. How come you and only you, among all these students here, have raised any objection to my teaching?"

"That's easy. Most of the other students are cowards and brown nosers."

"Brown nosers? What do you mean?"

"These women are behaving as they do to curry favor so they can get a good grade from you. They are brown nosers, pure and simple. Most women students, in my experience, are brown nosers."

"What say we put your assertion, your conjecture, to a test, Hodge? Sorry, I keep calling you by your first name. What's your last name?"

"Hootman."

"First, we should have a clear definition, Mister Hootman. How are you defining brown noser?"

"A brown noser is a person who curries favor by figuratively kissing ass. As these people kiss ass, some brown stuff from the ass hole rubs off and plants itself on the nose. Hence, the moniker—brown noser."

"Many thanks, Mister Hootman, for the definition. Aristotle says to prove a fact, we first have to establish a criterion that we will accept as proving or disproving something. For instance, suppose we disagree on the truth of the statement, "Gaido's restaurant in Galveston is now serving oysters." But we agree to call the maitre'd and go by what he says. So we call, and the maitre'd says, "Yes, we are serving oysters." Hence, the fact is affirmed because it met the pre-agreed criterion. So, now I ask you, Mister Hootman, to agree to the criterion that we poll the class and see how many of them think they meet your definition of brown noser.

"How will you frame the question?" asked Hodge.

"I will simply ask how many in this class self-identify as a brown noser? OK?"

Hodge paused and scratched his head, looked around at us, seemed to be taking our measure, and said, "I prefer the question be stated, "Those of you who do not self-identify as a brown noser, raise your hand."

"OK. How about we ask the question my way and then your way? The results should be the same; Clark will count the hands. Raise your hand if you self-identify as a brown noser."

Multiple hands up, and Clark said he counted 57. Amazing! Fifty-seven out of about 200 is not the majority, so Hodge is proven wrong.

"See, Hootman, I was right, and you were wrong. The majority do not consider themselves brown nosers."

"Not so fast. Ask the question as I gave it to you."

Meph-foe frowned but nodded. "OK, How many of you do not self-identify as a brown noser? Raise your hand."

We didn't need Clark to count hands. Only two of us—Lorrie and myself (I'm Lollipop. Remember me? I'm the one, dear reader, who addresses you directly; I'm the one talking) had our hands up. Fancy that! I wonder whether my classmates really understood the reframed question. Who knows? It looks, this time, like Hodge won and Meph-foe lost. Or, at best, a toss-up. It is not good to be on the wrong side of the power curve. Woe is Hodge. Meph-foe bore the injuries of Hodge as best he could, but when Hodge ventured on insult about teaching, I am sure Meph-foe vowed revenge.

The bell rang, and we left Meph-foe quirked eyebrow, wide-eyed, dropped jaw, tight-lipped, and speechless, gripping the podium tightly. His was the classic face described in Darwin's 1872 book *The Expression of the Emotions in Man and Animals*. Meph-foe's face was the face of anger and hate. Trouble was coming and soon.

CHAPTER FIVE

PILLOW TALK

"Anthropologists have amply documented the ascetic, the misogynist, and the male homosocial orientation of warrior cultures, marked by their distance from women as by their bonds between men."

—David F. Noble

Hodge and I met at the box just before the deadline of 6 P.M. No other students were there. They probably deposited their papers already. Those brown nosers!

"You ready, Lollipop?"

"I have a question."

"What? Meph-foe said no questions."

"Just kidding. But I do have a question. How about we have sex before dinner? I am so horny. If I don't get laid soon, I'll go crazy."

"You mean more crazy. You're crazy already. Must be midcycle. Sex, OK, I'll think about it. But the usual sequence is feed, then fuck. We will be curiously out of step with mainstream America and normative dating, and when out of step with the norm, there usually follows chaos. Hey, wait! You said you usually don't go to bed on the first date."

"Hodge, "usually don't" means "sometimes do." Besides, this is date two. The first was in the cafeteria. And can I be on top?"

"Jesus, the first question is, are we to have sex? Then and only then do we decide who is on top. You are again out of sequence."

"Please."

"Do we need equipment?"

"I have an IUD."

"Any STD?"

"Nope."

"OK. Where?"

"Marie shares her apartment with me. She is a harmless drudge and a brown noser, so she will be there studying, and we will have no privacy."

"How about the library, then?"

"Hodge, get serious."

"Parking lot? Front lawn?"

"How about your place?"

"Ho ho ho. My place will shock you."

"I am well-grounded, and I have been around. Very little shocks me these days. Let's go."

* * * * *

Hodge and I headed down highway 146 to Miles Road, just south of route 96 in League City. We cruised about a half mile east along an oak tree-lined street with pavement even worse than any in Houston. My teeth were chattering, and my butt was getting sore with the bounces. Hodge's shocks must be taking a beating, the tires, the suspension too.

We entered an RV park on the south side, and the ride got worse—rougher as we wound around a petite swimming pool loaded with green algae and turned into a cul-de-sac next to a stagnant pond.

"Whew! What a lousy road. Correction, what lousy roads. How do you stand it? This place gives me the creeps. There must be 400 RVs jammed together. Do people live like this? Hard to believe this dump is in America. Probably plenty of mosquitos in the pond."

"Lollipop, that pond is so polluted even the mosquitos can't live there. The people here live hand-to-mouth in abject poverty. They are the great unwashed of America. They're on welfare, unemployment insurance, stimies, and disability payments. Subsisting really. Some have low-paying jobs in welding or construction, and some are just beggars. Each hook-up costs $450 a month, which ain't bad. The stoves work on propane which you have to buy yourself. The place is owned by five Muslim men and one woman who live in Vegas. The Galveston Appraisal District shows no property taxes, so someone up and spoke to the captain."

Note from editor: "spoke to the captain" is American slang for "bribed a public official for a favor."

* * * * *

Before I talk about our date and what happened in Hodge's camper (he did not live in an RV. His was a camper, much, much worse and much smaller than an RV), I will display Hodge's first paper and ask you, dear reader, to evaluate it and guess what Meph-foe thought about it and guess what grade Meph-foe gave the work. And then, I will display Meph-foe's comments.

Next, you will see and evaluate my paper and see the same for it. This is one of the many advantages of literature. You can get flashbacks, and you can get flashaheads. Here I want to flash ahead. Let's get this out of the way before we get to the sex and real juice of this chapter, which you recall was entitled *Pillow Talk*.

OK?

SAN JACINTO JUNIOR COLLEGE. WHY WOMEN SHOULD RULE THE WORLD, 101

Professor Dante Mephistopheles
Title: Examples of Antiwomen Literature
By Hodge Hootman

First story is about Eve, who brought misery to all mankind because of her wickedness, for which Jesus Christ Himself was sent by God the Father to suffer a terrible death on the cross to redeem us with his life's blood. Here expressly, you discover that woman is the cause of the loss of paradise for all mankind.

Comment: Oblivious misogyny. How likely is it for the God who created the entire universe to go apeshit about some woman eating the fruit of a tree? And, get this, how likely is it that the great God who created the entire universe could think of sacrificing his only son as the only way to make up for Eve's offense? Why didn't this great God just forgive the sin the way Jesus gave Peter the power to forgive sin: "DABO CLAVES REGNI CAELORUM. I give the keys to the kingdom of heaven (Jesus supposedly continued) whose sins you shall forgive, they are forgiven them, whose sins you shall retain, they are retained."

Next up, we have Samson, who lost his hair. His mistress cut it off with her scissors as he slept, through which treachery, he lost both his eyes and strength and fell into the hands of the Philistines.

Comment: Pure misogyny. How likely is it that a man's hair would hold the secret of his strength? The conclusion that appears from scripture is that woman is the enemy of strong men.

Even classical myths are against women: Hercules and Dejanira, who caused him to set fire to himself.

What about the troubles of Socrates? How Xantippe emptied a chamber pot over his head. The poor man sat still as if he had died, wiped his head, and dared only to say (somewhat enigmatically), "Before the thunder stops, the rain comes."

How about the story of Pasiphae, Queen of Crete? She conceived the Minotaur (Bull of Minos) after mating with the Cretan White Bull while she was hiding in a hollow cow that the Athenian inventor Daedalus built for her. The Minotaur was half human and half bull and was not a nice guy because he fed exclusively on human flesh.

Comment: Obvious misogyny. According to the story of the animal nature of women, there can be no doubt. Pasiphae lusted for the White Cretan Bull and tricked the Bull into mating with her, thereby producing a monster.

More: Clytemnestra, the adulteress, murders her husband while he is taking a bath. Lesson: Women are killers. Watch out!

What about Latumius, who complained to his friend Arrius that a certain tree grew in his garden on which three wives had hung themselves. "Dear brother," said Arrius, "give me a root from this blessed tree, and I shall plant it in my garden."

And there are, in the more modern period, stories of wives who kill their husbands and then allow their lovers to sleep with them while the dead husband lies face up on the bedroom floor. Others had driven nails into their husband's brains and killed them. Some put poison in their husband's drinks and so forth.

Comment: Much literature is anti-women, as I have demonstrated. All these stories were written by men, and none were written by women. Given the chance, stories by women would probably be quite different.

C-

Mister Hootman: Have mercy on me and my soul. You were told to submit a paper no longer than two pages. Think of me. I have to read 400 student pages on a weekend. Most of the papers are complete, utter garbage. Do you realize what a task it is to read and grade such trash created by stupid, ignorant dumbbells? You are lucky I am in a good mood and gave you a C- instead of the F you deserve.

Your paper is poorly organized and a mess of disconnected ideas. And you stole a lot from *Chaucer's Canterbury Tales*. Did you think I would not pick up on *The Wife of Bath's Tale?* The thing that saved you is the fact you explained Pasiphae and what she did. *The Wife of Bath* just mentions Pasiphae and leaves us hanging if we didn't know what was what.

You might have mentioned more familiar examples of misogyny from Roman times, like how Sulpicius Gallus left his wife permanently because he caught her looking out the door bareheaded. And there was another Roman who divorced his wife because she went to a summer party without his permission. Then there was Salome, a deeply disturbed princess who fell head over heels for Jokanaan (also known as John the Baptist). When he rejected her advances, she performed the infamous and seductive Dance of the Seven Veils for King Herod in exchange for John's head on a platter! And you forgot to mention the essential contradiction: If Jesus redeemed humanity by his death on the cross, how come we all are not back in the garden of Eden enjoying the original paradise?

On the plus side, you did prove that much literature is anti-woman, very much so, and it is important to proclaim this fact. You also are probably correct that the literature is anti-woman because it has been mainly written by men.

By the way, DABO is the future tense, not present, as you translated it. Jesus supposedly said, "I will give you the keys to the kingdom of heaven. Not I give. Anyway, Jesus never said that because Jesus didn't speak Latin, he spoke Aramaic. One last point: Avoid errors in diction. Minotaur is *not a nice guy* hits the reader as a descent into slang, as does the word *apeshit*.

* * * * *

Lollipop talking now: Ugh! Poor Hodge. Meph-foe took it out on him because he didn't like Hodge's cockiness. What do you think? Hodge is disorganized, but he did make some important points, so I think his grade should have been higher, maybe even a C+.

Next comes my paper. See what you think.

SAN JACINTO JUNIOR COLLEGE. WHY WOMEN SHOULD RULE THE WORLD 101

Professor Dante Mephistopheles
This paper outlines a particular event in the women's movement to determine what was accomplished and what was not.
Title: Why Did They Not Burn Their Brassieres as Planned?
By Andzelika Dziedzic

In the swinging 60s, men burned their draft cards, and women burned their bras. Those actions have been referenced by many people in many discussions about gender equity. On one occasion, however, women were not permitted the privilege of burning their bras. Here's what they did instead:

On September 7, 1968, members of the New York Radical Women assembled outside the Miss America Pageant on New Jersey's famous Atlantic City boardwalk to protest the pageant. They claimed the pageant degraded women by promoting unrealistic standards of beauty and fake social expectations, which were, by their testimony, fueled by male lust and imagination.

What were they actually protesting? 1. Women were denied their own credit cards. 2. Women were denied the right to work if they were the slightest bit pregnant.

Originally, it had been planned to burn bras as a kind of public statement about their discontents. Makeup was to be trashed, and Playboy magazines ripped to pieces and burned. Local police shut down some of the stunts, citing fire hazards and specifically the danger that the famous boardwalk might go up in flames. Instead, the group hauled out a "FREEDOM TRASH CAN" into which they threw under panties, bras, cookware, high heel shoes, wigs, tampons, issues of Playboy and Hustler, and many other such items that participants deemed "instruments of female torture." The group crowned a sheep in mockery, comparing the Miss America Pageant participants to county fair show animals.

Some women thought the trash can idea overshadowed the event's larger message, but it wasn't all bad—the famed protest helped catapult the women's equality movement into mainstream America. Women eventually did get their own credit cards, and most were allowed to work if the pregnancy did not interfere with their effectiveness, their own health, and the health of the fetus. The pageant abolished the swimsuit competition in 2018, and in 2020, looks are no longer considered in judging. Bert Parks was out of a job, and we would no longer hear him sing, "There she goes, Miss America, your ideal."

The negative: Many believe the pageant's highlighted Swim Suit competition led many women to get silicone breast implants which, according to the FDA, caused sicknesses, deformed breasts, lymphoma, and some deaths.

A- Congratulations!

Very nice work. Full of interesting details and clear, coherent writing, writing almost at a semiprofessional level.

Our society is unspeakably cruel to women, shaming them for their age, their looks, their weight, their height, their voice, their hair, their clothes, and their makeup—all the result of patriarchy. Our society is not post-gender any more than it is post-racist.

You did the right thing picking on the Miss America Pageant, one of the best examples of misogyny in history. Where else could you find such a perfect example of sexism and racism? The pageant, in form and substance, fits the pattern of an auction of female slaves.

You may wish to expand your study by looking at the reign of Bess Meyerson as Miss America. In 1945, she was the first Jewish Miss America. Directors of the pageant encouraged her to change her name to Bess Meredith or Bess Merrick, but she refused. After winning, she received few endorsements. She was unable to stay in certain hotels, which had signs: No Colored, No Jews, No Dogs. Bess resigned and joined the anti-defamation league. She toured the country lecturing on how antisemitic America is and was and, of course, did not spare the pageant.

Also, look at the reign of Venessa Williams, who received multiple death threats and lots of hate mail. She was the first black Miss America and had to resign because of the (unauthorized?) publication of her nude photos in *Penthouse*. What a country!

When CEO Beck changed the pageant rules about age, previous pregnancy, divorce, and so forth, he was fired, and the old rules were reinstated.

Suggestions: Don't tell what your essay is about. That is an attempt at thought control. Let the writing speak for itself and let your reader judge it and decide what to take away and what not. Just put your title in bold, and don't identify it as the title. In other words, do not use the word title. Just write it.

WHY THEY DID NOT, ETC.

And avoid prejudicial words like swinging 60s. That has become a trite commonplace of vague and unclear meaning. Instead of mentioning *other instruments of female torture*, it is better just to state what they actually were and what was actually thrown in the trash can, including false eyelashes, hairspray, girdles, and corsets. Factual details are very important in journalism. They make the assertions believable. But stick to the truth and do not ad-lib or exaggerate. I doubt the women threw in tampons. You made that up. Didn't you?

Watch your use of adjectives. They frequently blur meaning. There is a difference between unrealistic standards and just plain standards. There is a difference between fake social expectations and just plain expectations. Thus, consider my rewrite: "promoting standards of beauty and expectations which were, by their testimony, fueled by lust." Adjectives often evade meaning or produce vague meaning. Example: We all know what justice is but what's *social* justice? We all know what racism is, but what's *systemic* racism?

Patch up your piece and send it to a magazine. Don't accept less than $200 in payment. Include a picture of the Freedom Trash Can:

For your term paper, you might look at the variety of plastic surgeries offered to women to change them to look like some idealized babe. The list is enormous and designed to make women ashamed of their bodies. Rhinoplasty for your too-big or too-little or too-deformed nose. Abdominal recontouring for those who think the little rim of fat is the cause of their troubles and difficulties with their husband. On and on: Stomach stapling. Eye lift. Neck pull. Cheek implant. Ear pinning. Leech lipo. Mustard gas face peel. Vaginal rejuvenation. Fingernail extension. Forehead reduction. Shoulder lifts. Spine straightening. Laser hair removal. Breast augmentation. Breast reduction. Lip injection with collagen from free-range chickens. Booty and hip package.

Take a look at the advertisements. They are disgusting. Tits so small you don't know they are there? Bad deep acne scars? Peter Lorre eyes?

Hi. I am Doctor Hamilton, a board-certified plastic surgeon. I PROMISE you I will change your life. Ours is a visual culture. Beauty counts and is a major calling card in this wide world. If you look good, the world will be good to you. Beauty comes with privileges and rewards. *Special payment programs are available. No credit check. This month only: Marriage saver special: Breasts, butt, lips, and hips for only $50,695.*

In my office, I have a full-color ad from TheSilicone.MD that shows patient pictures with before and after butt lift, nose job, tummy lipo, and so forth. All patients are women, of course, in various stages of undress. With TheSilicone.MD, there is no credit check and no interest. The payment plan is $1,500 down, $250/ month, and pay after your surgery. Apply online to FinanceMy-PlasticSurgery.com

Those are just some ideas and suggestions for what you might work on. All in all, you did a fine job on the paper. I would like you to come to my office some afternoon for further discussion and, perhaps if you like, a glass or two of sherry. Clark knows about your invitation. He was unhappy about it, so just disregard his sour face and come when you can come. Come when you can come.

* * * * *

And that was it, dear reader. The very moment I finished reading Meph-foe's comments, I loved him, and I was in love with him. What a great, great man! Then and there, I resolved that if this great professor needed anything from me, I would consider it an honor and a privilege to oblige him in any way he wished. How perceptive he was to figure out that tampons were not thrown in the freedom trash can. He was right: I made that up. I don't know why I made it up. I don't like tampons. Most women don't like them. But we need them.

Right?

* * * * *

Hodge's camper was surrounded by a brown wooden fence ten feet tall that gave the illusion of privacy. There were signs saying surveillance videos were in operation, but of course, there were no videos and no video. A sign on the fence and a sign on the door said beware of the dog, but there was no dog.

The strong metal door with three locks opened right into a small claustrophobic room, smaller than the bathroom in Marie's apartment.

"Hodge, this room and this camper are an embarrassment. Is it government issue?"

"It's bad, and this RV park is a dump, but it is not so bad for a down-on-his-luck San Jacinto Junior College student who, some months, has to borrow money to pay the rent."

This single room was Hodge Hootman's kitchen, study, living room, laundry room, and dinette. There was a small table in the far corner and a bookcase with two books. That was the library. Two small windows adorned the west wall. They were covered by dusty Venetian blinds. I pulled the lift cord to take a look, and the head box, tilt tube, cradle, and all fell forward and hit the floor. Blam!

"Sorry."

"No problem. I didn't like them anyway."

On the east side, a closet opened to the toilet. This was cramped quarters, and I had to pull my legs close in to take a pee. If this was a bathroom, it seemed constructed for a race of smaller humans. There were big mirrors on the north and south sides to make the bathroom look bigger than it was. So, when you sat to take a shit or a pee, you were treated to multiple images of yourself extending to infinity.

Hodge said to put no paper in the toilet because it gets clogged. And it didn't flush right, either. It was one of those that had a flush handle suspended a foot and a half above the floor. Hodge had to come in and kick it three times to get it to flush.

"To flush, you have to kick it with your foot. It flushes if you push real hard three times."

"Just put the toilet paper in the plastic bag next to the bowl. I'll take care of it."

Suddenly, the room and the whole camper began to shake.

"What the hell?"

"Just a truck passing in front. The rumbling noise will get louder and louder, crescendo style, and the vibrations will grow and recede and then die down. Truck shakes are part of the scene, and after a few weeks, you get used to them and actually miss them when they don't appear."

"Hodge, your camper smells of mildew, molds, dust, old dinners, bug spray, and je ne sais quoi. Open a window."

"Can't do. The windows have been painted shut. You know, Lollipop, before I would take the scouts on a camping trip, I gave them my routine talk: 'Scouts, for the next week, you are about to learn the most important lesson you will ever learn in life: And that is *How to Suffer*. Once you know how to suffer, everything else comes easy.' The trouble with you, Lollipop, is you never learned how to suffer."

To that talk of his, I said, "Talking about suffering, let's get the show on the road. Where's the bed? Let's fuck. Take me out of my current suffering."

Hodge pointed to a closed door to the right of the entrance. Voila! The bedroom was as large if not larger than the other room, and it was air-conditioned. The bed was a Queen with beautiful blue covers. There were two fleecy white pillows between which was a stuffy black bear called Bearington. There were no windows, so we had the privacy we sought. And the door locked.

"I'll be on top first. Then you can decide what position is next. I like doggy style, but conventional missionary is fine with me."

"Lollipop, why are you doing this? I know you don't love me. What's the deal?"

"Hodge, I do love you in my fashion, but mainly I need to screw for biological reasons, and I like the thrill of orgasm. No more talk. Let's fuck. But don't enter me until I say I'm ready. I'm hot but not yet wet."

I pushed Hodge onto the bed and jumped on top, pulled his belt off, his pants and underpants down. He had a good one. I lifted my skirt and tried to mount.

"What, no panties."

"I took them off in the car. You didn't notice because you were trying to avoid the potholes. I had to get ready for action."

I rode Hodge hard and got where I wanted to go in a matter of minutes. He didn't come, but he did stay erect. I like a man who takes his time.

The relief, the tenderness, the moisture, the electricity, the fragrant loveliness of the whole thing stirred me strangely. I was in his arms now, and I didn't care who bothered or what happened. He is beautiful, and I love him, and I knew I was happy and was willing to die. I cannot adequately describe what kind of joy I felt since it only can be experienced; she who has experienced it knows it.

We switched positions. His warm body was on me, aching for me, and I was aching for him. He was moaning in a solid animal health that glowed and glowed, and I glowed down there where women ought to glow. I grabbed his ass with all my might. You can't forget an ass like that, slightly wrinkled but fine, a real solid fact. He shuddered with a bright, grasping orgasm, a big one, much bigger than I have known with other men. I knew I could fuck him forever on and on, forever pushing myself into him. I wanted him to spill his self into me. I wanted to live with him. I wanted to marry him. I wanted to have children with him.

We napped. Then the camper shook and vibrated with a new truck.

"Our love makes the earth shake. Lollipop, I have never ever been kissed or loved like that. You are the best. No one can touch you. That was passion, the real deal. Thanks a million."

"Hodge, let's get married."

"And live on what? Let me give you a dose of reality. I live, like so many here, from hand to mouth. Three times a week, I get up at 5:00 A.M. and go to the food handout at Kroeger on Space Center. When the food outdates, they give it to us, the needy. Other days, I attend rounds at Methodist Hospital on NASA Road 1. They have grand rounds in medicine. Surgery and pediatric and always have lots of pizza and coffee. Saturday cardiology rounds are the best because they are catered. Yummy!

"The local churches stopped giving out food because there were too many of us and too many fist fights. The Bay Area Community Center stopped giving out ham and cheese sandwiches on Fridays because too many people showed up, and 100 sandwiches disappeared in minutes, leaving many people hungry, discontented, and angry. The sandwiches had very little ham and cheese, and the bread was stale. That was another problem—food given away is never that great, never Trader Vic's. Furthermore, Lollipop, the only way I pay the $450 a month rent on this camper is my job as a Murphy Man."

"Murphy Man?"

"Yes, Murphy Man. You won't like it, but I'll tell you anyway. This is how I make a living:

"I stand outside the George H. Brown convention center in downtown Houston and look for a mark. Usually, he is well dressed and attending a convention of dentists, lawyers, teachers, engineers, or some political group—the Trumpers are the best marks. If they believe Trump's shit, they will believe anything.

"When I find the mark, I get acquainted with small talk. How are you? New in town? Like Houston? What do you do? Are you attending the Trump group—wonderful people them, really know how to set this country straight. Not 'Make America Great' anymore. Now it's 'Save America.' And so forth. Most men are even more susceptible to flattery than are women, believe it or not.

"Then comes the crucial question: Are you interested in some nookie? Want to get something you don't get at home? Entirely safe and clean, guaranteed. After the usual hesitation, I ask, "What's your pleasure? Suck or fuck? What position? How about color?

Got yellow fever? I have a real nice chink who knows all the tricks. Or maybe you want to go black. Once you go black, you won't go back. I show some pictures on my phone. Pictures I copied out of Hustler. Their eyes pop out. Men are so bad. I have a feeling they think with their dicks more than they think with their brains. Usually, after the pictures, I get the nod and the big OK. All of them so far have always wanted just plain vanilla. Even the black guys want white. Of course, I tell him the dame involved does exactly what the mark says he would like her to do. A male fantasy come true. Gullible—thy name is man. The fantasy is the come-on; every con has a come-on. When it looks appropriate, I offer outfits—French maid, female cop, high school cheerleader, Dominican nun, go-go dancer, and Librarian. The engineers want the librarian. Trumpers go for go-go.

"So, after the mark makes his choices, we are in business. Time for the payoff.

"I explain. The woman is in a room in the Four Seasons Hotel right down there (I point to the Four Seasons). She is waiting for you. We use a nice respectable hotel, so there is no trouble. Get it? Another nod and usually a smile. But the room is $175, and the woman is $225, and my fee for arranging all this fun is $50, making a grand total of $450.

"The Trumpers have the cash. Some others, particularly the teachers, have to use the cash machine, which is conveniently situated right at the entrance to the convention center. None of this ever worked with the convention of the Texas Medical Society or the American Medical Association. The docs just say, 'Thanks, Buddy. I get plenty at home, and I need a rest.'"

"Next, the mark and I go to the second-floor lounge in the Four Seasons Hotel and have a drink of champagne, which the hotel has there for its guests. This is a first-class hotel. Then, I excuse myself and tell the mark I have to square things with the lady. Don't forget, I tell him, payment directly for sex is a no-no in this fair city. The money will have to come to me, and then I take care of her. Furthermore, I tell him, do not tip or leave any money for her. That is a big no-no. That could get us in big legal trouble. And if she asks for $100 for a haircut, or a subway fare, or to buy her cat some cat food, just say no. Explain that I strictly forbade you to give her money and tell her the reasons. She knows this, but it won't hurt to remind her.

"Now, I take the money and leave and return in five minutes with the report that the lady needs ten minutes to freshen up. Wait here, I say, for ten minutes by the clock. Then go to room 402 and say Mickey sent me. That's the password. OK? Mickey sent me.

"That puts the block in place. Cool setup, right? Ten minutes gives me time to escape. The parking garage next door connects to the second-floor lounge via a pedestrian bridge. I'm in my car in two minutes and away. My escape is perfect.

"The mark goes to 402—maybe. I don't even know if there is a room 402. Sometimes I imagine an elderly pair of grandparent types answering and wondering what the hell is going on. Anyway, there's no chance the mark would go to the cops because what he did is shameful and probably illegal. The scandal, if it got back home, might break his happy marriage, hurt his reputation, damage his good name, and so forth. All his actions are constrained by circumstances, blocked beyond his control. Pretty cool, right?"

"Hodge, you're a genius. How did you ever think this up?"

"I didn't. I read it in a book about scams. It's one of the classics like the pedigree dog scam, or Florida real estate underwater, or fake gold, which is bricks painted gold, ancient Egyptian antiques made yesterday, beautiful clear green emeralds that were the bottom of a Heineken bottle, and so forth. P.T. Barnum said a sucker was born every minute. That is wrong. More like every second."

"Did you ever try it on a woman?"

"Are you kidding? Women wouldn't fall for such nonsense. If I tried it on a woman, she would probably hit me on the head with her Louis Vuitton or call the cops or make a scene."

"This Murphy Man profession sounds just right for you and will provide us with a nice living. If you don't want to marry, I can just move in, and we can see if things work out. I can help with your homework. I can do the laundry, make breakfast, be your personal sex slave. Let's try. If we don't get along, we just quit with no hard feelings on either side. Please say yes."

"OK, we'll give it a try. You might pick up some dough helping our most prosperous resident, Claudia Couvert. When our welfare kids needed money to register for Bay Area Texas Baseball (ages three thru 18), she came through for them, nine kids at $150 each. The fee includes jersey, pants, cap, socks, and belt. Claudia told them: 'Kids, washing cars, raking leaves, bake sales, lemonade stands, and so forth are for chumps. If you really want to make money, try porn.'"

"She films right here in the park. Her most famous film is *The Abduction of Giselle Viper*, which Adult News said made revenge look ever so sweet.

"She has approached me several times because she says I look terribly handsome, able-bodied, and well-disposed for a career in the adult film industry. She says we can show those mideast terrorists what they are missing."

Me: "Child pornography is strictly against the law, and the penalties are terrible."

"Claudia isn't stupid. All actors are 18 or older. The kids work the cameras, handle the sound, adjust the lighting, edit content, work the computers, upload onto the internet, and maintain the website. When it comes to devices, kids are unbeatable."

"I told Claudia no. Porn is not my jam. Too much work. The Murphy game is more my style. Claudia also has a business on the side for willing young women. She says, 'Why give it away when you can make it pay?' She adds, 'The only difference between my girls and the average housewife is my girls give a man his money's worth.'"

"How long has she been in business?"

"Three years."

"Wow! She probably has enough money to buy a baseball team, and she might help finance a special project I have in mind, the liberation of women and the final solution to the global problem of severe unmitigated violence. We need money to buy weapons for the takeover. We need money for the biological research I have in mind. I'll talk to her."

"Fat chance of that. She is a shy, intellectually distant, pale woman with an air of not being there—a character right out of Chekov with an air of mournful abstraction. Unlike most Chekov characters, she appears to have taken the vow of silence and goes out of her way not to socialize with anyone who isn't a business interest. She does like kids, and she is four plus pro-women, so you might get somewhere with that angle. Her motto is 'When the lower classes are in need, I am always there for them.' The best time to hit on her is at the baseball complex on highway three. She is always there Saturday mornings cheering the kids."

* * * * *

That night, we didn't go out for dinner. Hodge made some special spaghetti, and then we hit the hay again, alternating love and sleep. There was some good pillow talk when I asked why he was taking the course.

"I have come to realize that most of the trouble in this wide world is caused by men, and if men were removed from power and women put in their place, we would all be better off, and civilization would be saved. The real question is how to do it, and that is what I am trying to figure out."

"Hodge darling, that's exactly how I feel. As I see it, the key is to figure out how men got power and then copy their methods. When they failed at some attempt to seize power, like January 6th, we need to study what went wrong and think of how to fix it. I am not exaggerating when I say I feel the entire health of humanity depends on avulsing men from power, and I firmly believe the entire health of the planet, our only home in space, depends on women saving civilization."

* * * * *

We continued our lovemaking, alternating sex and sleep while Bearington watched. I dreamed of a brave new world without masculine power.

It was the end of a great day. And the beginning of our secret society for the overthrow of male government. I mark the day with a white stone. Women must take over. But how and when? I got some leads—Claudia is one. Hodge is the other.

CHAPTER SIX

LECTURE THREE

"All along the rail, there were faces; in the portholes, there were faces. Leeward, a stale smell came in from the tubby steamer that rode at anchor with the yellow quarantine flag drooping at the foremast."

"'I'd give a million dollars,' said the old man resting on his oars, 'to know what they come for.'"

"'Just for that pop,' said the young man who sat in the stern. 'Ain't it the land of opportunity?'"

—John Dos Passos, Manhattan Transfer

"Welcome back," said Meph-foe with a grin.

Yee, gods! His hair and mustache were now deep dark, jet black. He no longer looked distinguished, more like a rake or a rounder. Meph-foe touched his hair, smiled, and shrugged his shoulders.

"And good afternoon. Thank you for coming. I hope you like my new look. Clark suggested I try to look younger.

"Before we get into the lecture, I wish to apologize for my behavior and for the offensive things I said in the last lecture. Some of you were justly offended and complained to the dean.

"Gertrude, the woman who objected to my not believing in God, has had her full tuition refunded and has dropped the course even though it was offered to her free of charge. I also wish to apologize to Mr. Hootman.

"He had, according to the dean, a perfect right to express his ideas and interest, although simple and simplistic. My problem was I had prepared a lecture and had a clear idea in my own mind what needed to be said. His questions and comments produced a kind of resentment in me that I now fully acknowledge as a character fault which I need to work on to prevent such things from happening again."

"Apropos of complaints, two of them stood out: Students said I used foul language. I told dean Mary McDonald that that was a goddamn fucking lie. She laughed. Students said I was too liberal. Mary said in this day and age it was not possible to be too liberal. She said, "Tell the students: 'You have a choice in elections: You can vote for the Democrats or you can vote for the lunatics.'""

Meph-foe paused, looked around the room, smiled, and acknowledged the applauses. Many of us cheered and stamped our feet. Some were even standing and clapping.

"My wish to you all is that you first tell me about your concerns before you go to the administration. My job here is not secure, and I plead with you to first talk to me, and then if you are not happy and not satisfied, talk to the dean. The dean has her share of problems, and she probably would welcome more time to deal with those problems than with the discontent of students. As for me, I am trying to earn a living in an uncertain world. I am not fit for any other occupation but teaching, and from the number of student complaints on my record so far, there is a question of whether I am fit for that.

"Let's review what we learned from the last lecture. Review time is never wasted. Don't take notes. I have decided there will be no tests in this course. Your final grade will be based on the quality of your papers, probably an average of the top two. So, there will be a midterm paper and an end-term paper, and that's it. No pesky quizzes or tests."

Meph-foe paused, looked around the room, smiled, and acknowledged the applauses. Again, many of us cheered and stamped our feet. Some were even standing and clapping. It was a reprise of what had just happened a few minutes ago. If he was trying to curry favor, he was getting it.

"Last lecture, we learned from Hodge's example not to sleep in class. We discussed the national problem of gun violence and its root cause, namely, men. We learned that a statement is a sentence that makes a definite claim, and we learned how to prove a statement true or false by deciding the criterion to be used. The Supreme Court's decision in Carson v. Brown occupied most of the discussion with Mr. Hootman seemingly defending the court."

Hodge stood up. "That's a lie. My comments were about your teaching and your exaggeration of the impact of the decision on the taxpayers of Maine. I did not defend the Supreme Court. In fact, I condemn the decision and strongly condemn the other decisions entirely. The Supreme Court is an anachronism, antipathetic to change, cathectic, and antichretic—a Model T Ford on the speedway unable to keep up with more modern machines, completely outdated. Using the term *court* for the Supreme Court is catachrestic."

Hodge was in the way, so I couldn't see Meph-foe's face, but I could imagine it, and so can you. I tried to copy the big words to look them up.

"Many thanks for your comment, Hodge. I shall take it under advisement. I did use the weasel word *seemingly*. Your corrections and comments are welcome."

"In the last lecture, we also learned the geographic location of Patagonia, the art of argument, and who to blame when a house is poorly constructed or Texas gets frozen. And that ends my review. Reviews are never wasted, never. They cement the memory. Review often, even what you think you know cold. Today we continue our analysis of the Extreme Court's June decisions.

Argument: Dobbs v. Jackson Whole Women's Health Organization (June 24). The court overturned Roe v. Wade, stripping away women's bodily autonomy and giving states the power to force women to give birth against their will.

Objection 1. It would seem the ruling was not the act of a secular court but the act of a religious tribunal. The five justices who ruled to take away women's right to abortion did not do so due to any fact-based debate about when human life begins or any good faith interpretation of the constitution, or any consideration of how abortion, in some cases, is medically necessary to save the woman's life. No, the Supreme Court is inviting religious dogma to override the rights, health, and lives of women.

Objection 2. It would seem the Supreme Court deceptively used its interpretation of the constitution to impose religious dogma on the entire nation, reversing two previous decisions the Supreme Court had made on this issue.

Objection 3. It would seem millions of women are now condemned to a loss of what should be a universal right of bodily autonomy and self-determination. Their intrusion of the police power of the state into the most intimate areas of one's private life marks the beginning of a new authoritarian era.

Objection 4. It would seem we must do whatever we can to restore the precious freedom that the court destroyed. To make matters worse, one justice signaled that the court is by no means finished with taking away American rights to suit their particular religious viewpoint. Justice Thomas wrote, "the court should reconsider all of this court's substantive due process precedents such as the rights to contraception and for same-sex couples to marry or even have sex."

Objection 5. It would appear the court has dragged this country founded on enlightenment ideals back into the dark ages.

"Any questions? Comments?"

Clark passed around a mic, and many students had their say about how they felt. One comment was particularly interesting. She said the Texas legislature passed Bill 8, saying, among other things, that preventing abortion was saving the lives of women because abortion can result in serious harm to the mother, even death.

Meph-foe shouted back, "The wheels fell off that argument when the New England Journal of Medicine published the adverse effects of legal abortion versus the death rate from the complications of pregnancy and delivery. The actual figures are 0.41 per 100,000 abortions and 23.8 per 100,000 live births, the worst record in the industrial nations of the world. Reference: New England Journal of Medicine 387:4 June 28, 2022, page 367. For that reason, and here I am quoting the New England Journal directly, "By abolishing long-standing legal protections, the U.S. Supreme Court's reversal of Roe v. Wade serves American families poorly, putting their health, safety, finances, and futures at risk. In view of the predictable consequences, the editors of the New England Journal of Medicine strongly condemn the United States Supreme Court's decision. Reference ibid. page 368."

Meph-foe suddenly had a frightened expression on his face, stopped talking, and collapsed onto the podium. Clark rushed to his aid, and so did one of the nurses in our group. They put Meph-foe supine and elevated his legs.

About three minutes later, he came to, dazed but himself. The nurse said his nail beds were pale, and so were his eyelids. She thought he was anemic and told the professor, "Get your blood checked."

Meph-foe dragged himself to his feet. "I feel dizzy and weak. In view of what has happened—I think I fainted. Class is dismissed.

We will continue the discussion next time with Kennedy v. Bremerton School District (June 27), wherein the court made it legal for a public school football coach to pray in public after a game. Part of free speech. So, you are free to pray and free to pray at public expense, but you are not free to have an abortion. Think about that! You ladies should be screaming."

* * * * *

I was finishing my notes and drew a heavy line under "<u>you should be screaming</u>" when I looked up to see Clark was coming down the aisle unmistakably toward me.

"Are you Andzelika Dziedzic?"

"Yes"

"Meph wants to see you," Clark said with a disgruntled expression, "in his office."

"What? Me? Are you sure?"

Clark shook his head and said, "Yes," with what looked like a sneer. "He wants you now!"

"What on earth! I didn't do anything. Why me?"

No answer from Clark. Instead, he just turned abruptly and left.

I gathered my things—and at the doorway, looked up and down the hall, trying to catch Clark again. But he was nowhere.

This was it. He was paying attention to me. To me! My chance to get to know the prof personally. I slipped into the girls' lounge, put down the books, and got out the comb and makeup. "What a chance," I kept thinking as I combed my hair briskly and finally spent an unusual amount of time adjusting the hair and putting on lipstick. What a silly thing is lipstick. It really is just a colored glue. What's the purpose? Damn. I should have spent time in the library to have something intelligent to say. Hodge! It was his fault. It was his fault. I don't know anything. Looking in the mirror, I decided I needed some eyeshadow to make me look older, more mature. Better darken the eyelashes a bit too. I pinched my cheeks for more color. Thank God I was wearing a tight red sweater that made my chest charms stand out. Not as much as Lorrie, who is stacked, but enough to make the right impression. Too bad there is no time to get really prepared. I could have used some lavishly embroidered pink panties. Come to think of it. Panties are surplus. I took them off and put them in my pocketbook. The final touch was a splash of *Intimate* by Revlon, one of my favorite perfumes.

At last, I was ready. I left the lounge and walked down the hall to the professor's office. I knocked on the door and heard at once the voice I loved and admired, his voice. Dear me, he has me hook, line, and sinker.

"Come in, come in. Come in, my dear, come in."

His office was exactly what Lorrie had described, small, dark, and dusty. Kind of claustrophobic. Books lined the walls from floor to ceiling, except for a small window that overlooks the parking lot and a door on the north side that led to another room. Meph-foe's desk, cluttered with papers, was large and old-fashioned with that cover that rotates and folds down. There's a dark blue couch by the south wall, a small table in the center of the room on which was, you guessed it, a bottle of sherry.

"My dear, I was just having my afternoon drop of sherry. I hope you will join me."

His face was wonderful, full of cheer, energy, and life, but very pale. What a lovely man. Impossibly handsome. I wanted to jump on him then and there and kiss and hug him to pieces. I had it bad. No question.

"OK. But I usually don't drink before five. The sun is too high over the yardarm. But 'usually don't' means 'sometimes do.'"

I was trying to look smart and impress the prof. And he was definitely coming along. He poured a glass, smiling and leering at my chest. Putting out for him was easy. I was in love, and who can explain love? Better to just live it. Right?

"Many thanks for coming. I like to get to know my students, make them feel at home and comfortable. You are looking great. I like to take a drop in the afternoons. It's much better than tea. Some people prefer tea. Not me. Too much trouble. Sherry for me. I like the way it looks—light brown. I like the way it smells—herbal. I like the way it tastes—slightly nutty, complex, and intriguing. I like the way it makes me feel—happy and relaxed. This one is from Jerez, Spain, fortified to 17.5%, a gift from the poet laureate Professor Loccul. It is not a good sherry. It is a great sherry." He held the glass out and looked at me with eyes of desire.

Holy cow! This is almost an exact replay of the Lorrie story. This is Meph-foe's M.O., his modus operandi. Next, he should introduce the Edgar Allan Poe skit. Damn! I should have read up on Poe so I would have something intelligent to say.

"Andzelika Dziedzic. What a name. Polish, right? You might consider changing it. My real name is Kumbar, from a small hick town in the Deccan, Indian Subcontinent. One of the great things about America—you can change your name at will. Why carry a name around like yours that few can say correctly? I didn't like my name, so I changed it to something I like. Something people will notice. Something they will remember. Immigrant too, right?"

"Yes"

"What's your story?" asked Meph as he poured another sherry for himself, held the glass up, and said, "A la tienne, to youth, to your youth, and to your beauty, and to your energy. You are the fresh chick just hatched from the egg. You are the future." And then, after having recited that passage from *Peter Pan*, he paused and quoted Shakespeare, "To joy and fresh new days of love."

"My story?"

"Yes, I love immigrant stories. Immigrants make this country great. They are the bold who had the guts to leave their routine boring life for adventure."

"Mine's routine. Pretty boring too."

Meph-foe refreshed my glass. The sherry was loosening me up, and what the hell? Before we got the show on the road, I would tell him the short version of my adventure. He may have been the type who wanted to know me before he, in the biblical sense, *knew* me.

"I was born in Panow, a Polish village near the Russian border. Father was a tailor. By Polish standards, we were well off. Father had been to America and came back with the most fantastic stories, which none of the village people believed. About telephones that you could use to talk to friends miles away and indoor toilets and lights that were not fire or candles. He decided to move the family to America in installments. I was the oldest of 13 children, a sister and 11 brothers, so I was selected to go first. He paid the transporter and took me to the next town, which was on the railway. After giving me a hug, he turned me over to the travel broker and left. The train rocked me to sleep. Just before Danzig, someone shook me awake. We had to get off. Some young men had not done their military service, so the border guards would have turned them back, and the guards might have spotted my fake papers and turned me back."

Meph sat on the blue couch and patted the area next to him. I sat. Don't tell me this was the protocol. Did he lock the door? We shouldn't do it here in his office. I wonder how many others have sat right here in this same situation. No matter. He was a great man, and I was ready to do whatever he wanted.

Meph put his hand out and turned it palm up as though to express some feeling (an abstract feeling), but finding that feeling ineffable, he let his hand drop onto my knee. He gave it a little squeeze before withdrawing his hand.

"You are top drawer, a real storyteller. Please continue."

He was giving me the eye and slipped his hand around my neck, and headed down to my right boob. My heart gave a little leap. He was handling me just as he handled Lorrie. I liked his looks and smiled at him. We're on our way. Should I tell him to lock the door? Someone could surprise us. Not good for his reputation, not good for mine. Meph refilled my glass. I continued my story.

"We went through some wet, dark, dirty tunnels into Germany. I was scared, but the transporter was well-paid and did a great job. Then to Bremen, where we got the ship. I got the penthouse suite— the top bunk, which became my bedroom, living room, dining room, and study. The food in steerage was worse than what we fed the animals at home in Poland. Mother had packed a potato sack full of salamis and cheese, so compared to the others, I ate well.

"Days went by. Then there was a big commotion on deck. Everyone rushed to the rail and began screaming and waving. I was certain we were sinking, but on an island was a colossal sculpture, the famous copper gift from the people of France. The statue is the figure of Libertas, the Roman Goddess of Liberty. A broken chain and shackle lie at her feet. Even thinking about it, I still get choked and teary. Now it means even more because she is a 'Mighty Woman, the New Colossus, the Mother of Exiles.'"

"One of the men grabbed me. 'Look!' He shouted in Yiddish. 'The American Lady! The Statue of Liberty!' And in that moment, I shouted as wildly as the rest of them. We had arrived at the climax—the Golden Land of Opportunity, the land of the free and the home of the brave."

Give me your tired, your poor, your huddled masses yearning to breathe free, the wretched refuse of your teeming shore. Send these, the homeless, the tempest-tossed to me. I lift my lamp beside the golden door."

I thought to myself: The more I tell my official story, the more it feels true.

Meph let out a gasp. "Oh, Loren, that was beautiful. I'm sure Emma Lazarus was no doubt thinking of Jewish refugees from Russia like you."

"I am not Loren. And I am not Russian. I'm Polish."

"I'm sorry. I meant Karen."

"I am not Karen either. I have that long Polish name—remember? (He was a little turned out and tipsy.) So just call me what my friends call me—Lollipop."

"Lollipop, what a sweet dear name. Lollipop, I am about to offer you a beautiful and thrilling privilege."

He looked at me expectantly, refilling my glass of sherry again. I was seeing two of him, one him and one that looked like his twin brother. I was having trouble following what he was saying. His voice came from far away. Was I drunk?

"My dear, there are bourbons (or did he say burdens) that are so deep and so—aching they must be satisfied."

I took another sip of sherry. I tried to look relaxed by leaning back but not yet supine. My mind was racing to find something intelligent to say, something smart and appropriate. I could think of nothing, for my mind was filled with a recurrent thought. A truly great man. I'm in the presence of a truly great man. This scene looks weird, dear reader. But remember, love is blind, and lovers cannot see the petty follies that they themselves commit. I am a woman in love. I smile, of course, and go on drinking sherry.

"You won't deny me," he pleaded. "I know you are too wise and too good to be selfish and not share yourself. You want the thrilling privilege of giving fully."

"Oh, professor, you had me that first lecture. I'll do whatever you want me to do. I'll be whatever you want me to be. It is an honor and a privilege to comfort you in any way you wish. Take me! Take me, please.! Take all of me!"

I was about to fling myself at him when the door burst open.

In came Clark, who had so begrudgingly conveyed the invitation to me. His eyes went wild, and his face went pale as he looked from Meph to me and back.

"Excuse me!" he said and made an acid face like a child rejecting the breast. He turned to leave. But Meph got up to stop him, grabbed his arm, and pulled.

"Wait, Clark. It's not what you think. It's only"– Meph-foe was crimson, clearly embarrassed. Clark had stopped at the half-opened door and looked directly at Meph.

"I'd better be going. You two have things to talk about. Important things, I'm sure."

"No, no, Clark," said Meph, collecting himself and letting go of Clark's arm. "Clark, go into the inner office. We need to talk."

Interesting. Clark looked at him, no longer pale but sulky and dark.

"Go," repeated Meph firmly. "I'll go with you. Come with me." He repeated gently, "Please come with me."

Meph-foe turned to me just before closing the inter-office door. "Excuse us for a minute. Clark needs me."

"Yes, of course."

I could hear some loud altercation, and then there was silence. There might have been a noise like a door slamming, so I assumed Clark left. I waited and waited, but Meph-foe did not return. I was wet and raring to go. What's the deal?

Selfish! What's wrong with you, Lollipop? I asked myself. Meph needs you and your consolations. You love him and would wait forever for this great man. I couldn't help the way I felt. I couldn't control the way I was about to behave.

Time went by. Clark had left, I thought. I needed to get back to do the laundry and the library and Hodge. I can't wait forever. I put my ear to the door and heard what were sobs and moans. And then I heard another sob and another moan that had come obviously from Meph. "I am coming, Dante, darling. I am coming," I whispered, and I opened the door.

Meph was on the floor on all fours with his butt up, and Clark was pounding him from behind. This was unnatural sex. I had read about it in novels and heard about men having sex with men, but this was the first time I had actually seen it. The floor was clothes-strewn, and both men stark naked. They were moaning and sobbing and groaning. They were not distracted from their intense scene, and they didn't notice me. Then Clark lashed out in a great frenzy, shaking all over. The big moment had arrived. He cried out and then fell limply on top of the professor, who collapsed to a prone position on the floor.

I closed the door quickly and exited down the hall. My head was clear enough to know I was seriously blotto. My arms and legs were out of control, flailing about, and I was wobbling side to side, hitting hallway walls and bouncing off. Things were double, especially in the distance. But if I closed either eye, the scene rearranged itself into a single vision. I was drunk and pie-eyed, but how could that happen with only five glasses of sherry? Somehow it did. There is no way I am driving to the RV park. Need to sleep it off in the student lounge. I had gotten older and a bit wiser. So far, the joke was all on me.

* * * * *

My affection for Meph-foe had altered.

I still loved him but not that much. I was just one of many in his stable that he would call to his office when he felt the need. I drank the sherry — like Lorrie and probably many others. For all I know, Meph-foe and Clark could be the Gulf Coast distributors of AIDS or Monkey Pox or both. They might be a public health hazard. From now on, I shall stick with Hodge. I shall be a safe sex Lolli-pop. Hodge and I shall be a safe-sex and sane-sex couple.

Meph-foe and Clark's secret was safe with me. Why stir the shit pot? Of course, I couldn't tell any woman in the class. Two women can keep a secret if and only if one of them is dead.

That Meph-foe was bisexual was a big surprise. But at the time, I had no idea of the even bigger surprise that was coming his way and ours.

CHAPTER SEVEN

A VOICE SAD AND PROPHETIC

"To be yourself in a universe which is constantly conspiring to make you something else is the greatest accomplishment."

—Emerson

"Welcome back. Thanks for coming. I hope you are having a nice day, and I hope it continues that way. As for me, I am feeling much better after a two-unit blood transfusion which has helped correct my anemia. It was foolish of me to disregard the shortness of breath I had just walking across the room. I now realize that was not normal, and I should have consulted doctors about that symptom.

"I am feeling worlds better. That's the good news."

Meph-foe continued with a voice now turned sad and prophetic, "The bad news is the doctors have found something wrong with my blood. Further tests are needed. Tomorrow morning, at M.D. Anderson Cancer Hospital, they will take a bone marrow biopsy and a bone marrow aspirate. Depending on the results, treatment may be needed, and this could have an adverse effect on the continuation of this course. If there is a pause, I wish to assign two books for you to read and digest:

"Book one: *A World Without Women: The Christian Clerical Culture of Western Science* by David F. Noble. Oxford University Press 1992. In this groundbreaking work, Noble provides the first full-scale investigation of the origins and implications of the masculine culture of western science. Correcting the notion that the culture of learning has always excluded women, Noble, a professor of history at York University in Toronto, shows that the advent of ascetic culture among Christian clerics from the late medieval period has led to male dominance over institutions of higher learning and to the exclusion of women. He demonstrates with multiple historic facts and details that women had not merely been marginalized and anathematized in the science-based civilization spawned by this ascetic culture, but he also shows how these attitudes remained intact through the Reformation and continue to exert a strong influence today.

"Read and weep about how women were burned at the stake for being witches. Church records, mainly court documents, of trials indicate the ladies were accused of changing into familiars, usually black cats, and flying around on brooms, as well as having had sexual intercourse with the devil himself. Signed confessions were used to prove guilt, even though such confessions were the product of duress and torture. It is expected that women would confess to anything under the influence of the rack, hoist, and red-hot pincers. Changing into black cats? Flying? As resourceful as women are, they cannot change themselves into black cats. Nor can they fly. Those things are not possible. Resourceful as women are, they cannot do the impossible.

"During the inquisition, whole German towns were emptied of women because all the women had been murdered by being burned at the stake. The alleged proof a woman was a witch is laughable by modern standards: A brown mole in the wrong place, an ectopic nipple, could spell doom. Witches were known to the church officials to float, whereas normal women were considered heavier and will sink. This led to the witch water test with a special chair designed to dip the accused in a river or lake. The specific gravity of a normal woman is such that the body will float, and all the women did float, proving the conjecture and supposedly proving their guilt.

"A World Without Women: The Christian Clerical Culture of Western Science by David F. Noble is an important book, a bold and provocative work. I recommend it without reservation or hesitation.

"Book two: *The Handmaid's Tale* by Margaret Atwood. Fawcett Crest 1985. Canadian poet Atwood has written a cautionary tale about how the moral majority of her day (now the radical right and the Trumpers) will control women's reproductive capacity. The novel gains power and effectiveness in view of the recent decisions of the U.S. Supreme Court. She takes many trends which exist today and stretches them to their logical and chilling conclusions. An excellent novel about the directions our government is taking. Read it while it is still allowed.

"Students, do a book review of either book as your midterm paper. Make sure your review is two pages and only two pages. Make sure it is typed and double-spaced. I was a nice guy with your first papers and did read some of them that exceeded two pages. I won't do that again.

"Now that you have your assignments, let's get to today's lecture. But first, a review. Review time is never wasted. It is important to review what you think you know cold as well as the material you don't know so well. Failure to review what you know cold may result in a special type of forgetting, which the psychologists have a special term for—restrictive forgetting. You forget because you restrict your review to the things you don't know well and neglect to review what you think you know well.

"Last time, we reviewed my many faults, including my use of bad language, my liberalism, and my disbelief in God. And we witnessed my collapse from exertion and anemia. The discussion was about Roe versus Wade and the Extreme Court's reversal of two previous Supreme Court decisions. We touched on the profound implications for the health of women in backwater states like Texas, where the radical right and the Trumpers and the country hicks hold sway. At the next dinner party, when the topic comes up, be sure to mention the exact case styling. That will give what you have to say an air of authority and power. The case was what?

I raised my hand. Meph-foe nodded. "Dobbs v. Jackson Whole Women's Health Organization. (June 24)."

"Very good, miss—I'm sorry, I forget your name."

"Call me Lollipop."

That was it. I finally spoke in class. Then and there, I decided I needed public speaking practice if I were to lead an avulsion that would end up with the world controlled by women, and I wanted to show the sisters here that you don't have to be shy or passive or a brown noser. You can speak out and express yourself. You can make a difference. Make history. Speak out.

So, I decided to get on my soapbox now that I seemed to have the floor. I don't recall exactly what I said, but it went something like:

Me: "Also important were decisions we did not have time to discuss. The court mocked scientific fact by obviating a modest and reasonable gun control law in New York despite research showing that gun control saves lives."

Meph-foe interrupted. "Obviating? Pretty fancy word. Definition, please."

"Write down the word, sir, and look it up tonight. That's what you told us to do when we were unclear about a word's meaning or flat-out didn't know.

"And, professor, please do not interrupt. I have definite ideas about what I want to say and how to say them."

I continued, "The court issued a body blow for environmental science. It struck down the implementation of a reasonable plan that allowed the EPA to regulate greenhouse emissions from existing power plants. Believe it or not, the court objected to the fact that the plan would have shifted production from coal to natural gas. Apparently, the justices found no support in the constitution for environmental regulation. They forgot, like so many GOPs, that this is the Age of Aquarius from now until 2050, during which astronomers predict a new age of human consciousness toward truth and reality. Times had changed. The notion that the constitution could contemplate climate change is ridiculous."

"Thank you. Very interesting points of view. Anything else you wish to lecture us about at glacial length, Lollipop?"

"Well, now that you mention it—yes. I think you and others are missing the big picture. You hit the details, get the trees clearly in focus, but miss the forest."

"Oh, do I? And what may I ask is the big picture? What forest have I missed? Enlighten me." Meph-foe signaled Clark for a glass of water. I wasn't fooled. Water isn't colored orange like sherry. He gulped it down. Drinking sherry in class is a no-no, but Meph has passed the devil-may-care post and is moving onward fast.

Me: "It's simple: The court is lost. Lost! They, the justices, are fuddy-duddies. The constitution, the law that governs the country, is a fossil, outmoded, and needs adjustment, massive adjustment. At the time the constitution was written, I don't know when, let's say, around 1787, women couldn't run for office or vote; they were shunned for even expressing political views. At the first federal census in 1770, nearly one person in six was a slave and was held as property. You talked about guns and how the court and some stupid people think the second amendment gives them the right to tote modern weapons. Ho ho ho. At the time the Bill of Rights was ratified, carrying a weapon meant, mostly, hauling around a lousy old musket that took ten minutes to load in hopes of shooting a rabbit for supper.

"What's the remedy? I don't know, but I think the nation must be considered a work in progress. We must recognize the constitution does not mention anything about same-sex marriage or abortion or contraception or iPhones or telephones or airplanes or space travel or stock markets or hydrogen bombs, and so forth. Modern times demand a more modern, more scientifically informed, more reasonable government guided by a more modern constitution. You agree?"

Meph-foe was leaning on the podium, chin in hands. Clark gave him a glass of the yellow whatever and a white pill. Meph-foe liked what he drank and looked happy, smacked his lips, and added, "Bravo. Right, oh, Lollipop. Class, you have just now seen the first flowering of pussy power. America and the Extreme Court are stuck with a government that worships a set of documents created by men, and only men, who had no idea about evolution, dinosaurs, hydrocarbons, and women's health. By the way, I have to compliment you, Lollipop, on your masterful presentation. Where did you learn to speak like that? Where did you learn to think like that? You're a gem. I couldn't have said it better myself. Really!"

"Yale, sir. I hold an A.B. and a Masters from Yale."

"Holy cow!" Meph-foe said with a puzzled look on his face. After a beat, he asked, "So how come you are in this rinky-dink junior college? Taking a course from a has-been, a completely washed-up and almost defunct professor like me. Tell me."

"Just lucky, Professor Mephistopheles. Just lucky."

* * * * *

And that was it—the first and last time I ever spoke in class, for it was the last class.

Regrets I have, just like that little French kid, Frantz, in Alphonse Daudet's famous short story *The Last Class*. It's change seen through the eyes of a child. Little Frantz wakes up one morning discovering the Germans have ordered from Berlin that all lessons shall be in German and not in French. The new teacher arrives tomorrow and this day marks the last class in French. Prussian forces under Otto van Bismarck captured Alsace and Lorraine and other parts of France in the War of 1870.

And so, little Frantz looks back with a kind of wistful regret about time wasted, opportunities lost, lessons missed, and so forth—all the written and spoken French he didn't learn. And he looks ahead with a kind of wistful regret about what he will not learn in the future, all the French he will never know, as the language of instruction switches from French to German.

The same mood of wistful regret overtakes me now. I'm sad, and I feel like crying. Life can be so cruel. I wish things had turned out differently, but alas, they never will. The past is completely closed. It cannot be changed or rearranged or undone. This was our last class. Meph-foe, like Monsieur Hamel, the teacher in *The Last Class*, bowed his head and said with a wave of his right hand, "That's all. Go."

The next time I saw Meph was in the M.D. Anderson Cancer Hospital. He was in bad shape, and he knew it. His major worry surprised me, and I am sure it will surprise you.

CHAPTER EIGHT

BAD KARMA AND HLA TISSUE ANTIGEN MISMATCH

"The most shocking fault of women is that they make the public the supreme judge of their lives."

—Stendhal

The University of Texas M.D. Anderson Cancer Center is the largest cancer center in the world. According to Newsweek, it is the best cancer center in the world, both as to cancer research and treatment. It is the number one recipient of cancer grants from the National Institutes of Health. If all of the foregoing is true, then the world and the United States have lots of work to do to improve things.

My first suggestion is to change the name of the hospital to something like The Andersen Hospital for Cancer and Allied Diseases. That way, people who came here and entered the hospital might at least have the hope they had an allied disease and not the dread disease, cancer.

The public waiting rooms and the public rooms, in general, should be larger, better lit, better cooled, better soundproofed, and better ventilated. The ground floor lobby was too crowded with people of all sizes, shapes, colors, ages, and nationalities. The place reeked with the smells of closely packed humanity, and the noise level exceeded the tolerance, I venture to say, of most humans. However, the old guy at the grand piano playing Beethoven's *Fur Elise* was a nice touch. I put a dollar in his bowl, and he either smiled at me, or he smiled at the cash, or both.

The purpose of my visit, as you, dear reader, probably guessed, was to find out if Meph-foe had any ideas about how to bring about the reign of women.

He was an in-patient on the fourth floor. The pavilion was the rotunda type, with the nurses' station in the center and the patient rooms radiating outward. Meph-foe had a nice clean single room with a window facing the street. The room was high enough so that the street noises were toned down but not so high that you couldn't still hear the kids having fun in the park.

The room looked like his office, only worse. It was a book-lined cave that smelled of himself, disinfectant, alcohol, the mephitic odor of feces, papers piled on papers, undusted old books, and yellow pages of manuscript handwritten in Meph-foe's hand. Disarray reigned in musty surrender to chaos. Meph-foe had all the trappings of a scholar because he was one.

He looked like himself, only less pale and more like something that had been swept up after a New Year's party. When I entered his room, he was asleep, supine, and propped up on three pillows. I didn't wake him. Instead, I sat at the bedside, patiently waiting and waiting, silent as a stone and as serious as a funeral director.

The intravenous was running in his right arm that was taped to a green board. The IV bottle read: Normal saline; the infusion machine was labeled IVAC. The monitor in back of the bed and higher than the bed board silently flashed lots of yellow squiggles that arrived in regular pulses, probably an electrocardiograph, which I couldn't read.

Suddenly, Meph's legs started shaking, and then his arms and then his whole body and then the whole bed and all the stuff.

Meph awoke screaming, "No, not that! No. No. Please no! A dung bug—no. A dung beetle, please, no, please. Egypt—not for me. Desert, no. Help!" He was gasping like a man ready to croak. A pause and then a loud scream: "HELP!"

I didn't realize a man could scream so effectively, but Meph-foe proved they could. Nurses must have heard him, but no one came.

I held his hand, pressed hard, and poked him hard in the ribs. "It's OK. Everything's OK," I shouted. "You are having a bad dream. Professor Dante Mephistopheles, wake up!"

He came to and stared intently at me. "Who are you? What's this (he is looking at the green IV board.) What? (He looked puzzled at the ceiling.) What's happening? Whose home is this? Am I back in the sanatorium?"

It dawned on him. "Ugh! The hospital. My room. And you are one of my students, Candy something, Candy Christian."

Candy was one of the students, alright. I didn't like her—she's a pussy and a silly mousey thing who wears bras that push her tits up. She puts out routinely but has nothing much in the clearstory. Her daddy drives her to class. She says, "I can drive, but since I don't have a license, I can't drive."

"Not Candy, professor. I'm Lollipop, one of your students, fifth row center, in back of Hodge Hootman."

"Hootman! That gadfly. Every class has a troublemaker. Hootman is mine—my gadfly. We all have our little crosses to carry. Hootman is mine. Why does a man take a course titled *Women's World: How Women Should Save Civilization?*"

"That is not the title of your course. The title is *Why Women Should Rule the World*. But how women should save the world is exactly what I want to know, what we want to know. Hodge Hootman is the same. He wants to know. His father is George Hootman, the director of the former IVF Institute of Houston affiliated with The Women's Place at Texas Children's Hospital."

"IVF?"

"Yes, in-vitro fertilization. The Hootman Clinic and Institute have suffered with Senate Bill 8 going into effect, and Doctor George has born the injuries of the Texas legislature as best he could, but when they ventured on Bill 8, ruining his whole professional career, he vowed revenge."

Meph made the inquiry face, dropped his jaw, and squinted his eyes. "George Hootman is a big-time doctor. Or was, until the jerks put him out of business. What the hell is the son of a big-time doctor doing in a small-time junior college?"

Me: "Doctor George and Planned Parenthood have been hit and hit hard. Hodge works with his father to try to do something. Your course offered hope. Texas, a dangerous place to be pregnant, is getting scarier. Texas now leads the nation in maternity ward closures and is dead last among the 50 states in maternal care. Women now have to flee Texas to get an abortion. The IVF Institute is closed because the state of Texas considers embryos humans entitled to official protection."

"That's stupid."

"Yes, stupid, but a fact. Since they say the embryos are individuals, they may be entitled to drive a truck, vote, and buy an AK-47. Who knows?"

"What a mess! Sorry!"

"Not as sorry as those without resources or support who will be forced to remain pregnant or seek abortion outside of the health care system. As usual, the blacks, Latinos, and indigenous will suffer the most. Devastating—that's what it is, Hodge, and I aim to fix it. Yet, how and when?"

Meph-foe looked up at the ceiling, scratched his head, and closed his eyes. What was he thinking?

"Lollipop, it's all over for me. The idea of the course was to focus attention on the problems of women. The solution is beyond me. Impossible, really. Men are too entrenched. Deposing them from power can't be done. The situation is hopeless and will remain hopeless for the next hundred years, at which time it will be worse. Soon I will be descending into the dust. Soon I will be among the strengthless dead on the other side of the grass. Get me a chocolate here, will you? My mouth is parched. I must have slept with my mouth opened."

Meph-foe's hand groped over the night table knocking over Clark's picture and then into the drawer, coming up with nothing. I couldn't find the chocolates either.

"The doctors were here this morning with their entourage of medical students, nurses, interns, fellows, residents, pharmacists, social workers, radiotherapists, oncologists, hematologists, chaplains, the medical humanist, and even the in-house lawyer. Quite a group! I wonder who is paying them. I hope not me. The head physician didn't mince words. He advised me to make a will for which they have an on-call in-house attorney right here in attendance (he pointed to Clancy, who waved hello), and then the doctor advised me to plan my funeral. Unfortunately, I would have to look elsewhere for a funeral planner as none were on call at the hospital. Too bad. There were three stiffs right here on this ward this morning. Lots of business for funeral planners! Reminds me of that Latin poet who remarked Simplicius used to be a physician; now he is an undertaker. What he used to do as a physician, he now does as an undertaker.

"The acute myeloblastic leukemia will probably go into remission with chemotherapy, but the remission will not last long, so they say I need a stem cell transplant to give me any chance of survival, and they emphasized the chance is a slim one. The HLA tissue antigen match from a non-related donor will probably cause graft versus host reaction and lots of trouble. Furthermore, they have some kind of vitality index that measures a patient's vitality. The higher the vitality, the better the chance of survival. Makes sense when you think of it. The healthier I am, the better I can withstand the poisons they will throw at me. The vitality index runs from zero, meaning you're dead, to 100, fully alive with no problem doing all the activities of daily living. An index of 80 is considered a good sign. Anything less predicts trouble. Mine is a miserable 47: High blood pressure, overweight, diabetes, liver problems—mainly bad luck."

Meph-foe had a pained expression on his face. His tone became softly probing, like a doctor trying to get to the bottom of a case history. "We can't even say our knowledge of death is shallow. There is no knowledge. There is only adumbration. All is not flatly knowable—disappointing, but true."

There it was, another oddity: Meph-foe was dying, and yet he ranted at our lack of knowledge of death. Meph, knotted and tangled, supplied more oddities than I could keep up with, and I am sure you, dear reader, are having the same trouble. I remained serious as an undertaker for a while and then had to say something.

"Professor Mephistopheles, death can't be as bad as it seems. It happens to everyone," I said, rubbing the side of my face. My eyes were irritated. Or was I crying? What I had said was cruel, but it was the truth. But God were we pathetic!

What would it be like to be dead? It was hard to imagine. Try to imagine it. You can't. Meph was right. We know so little about death, and yet it was and is the common experience of all life. My view is it is like being inside a book and no one reading it. What a pity!

The bed bent under Meph's weight as he shifted his buttocks like sacks. If I kept quiet, I was sure I would hear an elaboration. Meph loved to hear himself talk, and those who were about to die deserved to be listened to. You agree?

"I am not happy," he said. "I wanted to continue my research on the misogyny problem and perhaps find a solution or solutions. Serious thinking is needed. It all started around 400 A.D. with the cult of the virgin. What's so special about a virgin? The gospels of Matthew 13:55 and Mark 6:3 both say Jesus had four brothers, James and Judas, and I forget who else."

Me: "Joses and Simon."

"Yes, thank you. And Matthew and Mark say Jesus had sisters but do not name them. So, how could Mary be a virgin with so many children? Virgins don't give birth. That's an insult to women. It was impossible where and when Mary lived. Where was I?"

"We want to know how to fix the oppression of women, and we would welcome ideas about that from you."

"Visit next week, and I might have answers for you and Hodge. And I might not. Right now, it looks like women need to take control of the government by force. They may profit by studying the January 6th insurrection and plotting what went wrong and planning a correction. The larger problem, namely the complete extinction of all human males, seems impossible to solve under present technology. Men are by nature weaker biologically than women, so taking advantage of the inherent weakness is the way to go. But how?"

Meph stopped, stared at me, smiled, smacked his lips, thought of something, and continued.

"Lollipop, you are completely wrong. Yes, wrong! Wrong from the start. I have no fear of death. Death is completely natural and expected, and normal for someone like myself with acute leukemia. My worry is quite different. I am worried, worried sick, worried about what is going to happen to me after death."

Me: "The undiscovered country from whose bourn no traveler returns puzzles the will."

"Not at all. What puzzles me is what I will become after death. That's the real question. The nightmare I just had was about my return as a dung beetle to roll dung in the Egyptian desert for a lifetime. I am a Brahmin, a special type of Brahmin—a Kulin. Some two cycles ago, I must have developed remarkable karma. My reward was to be reborn, reincarnated, interesting word that— meaning into the flesh again, as a Brahmin, the top caste consisting of priests and intellectuals. This time around, my karma is not so good. Mistakes have been made, many mistakes.'

"Professor, you're kidding. You don't believe that crap. Do you?"

There's something hilarious about this, what Meph-foe is saying, but I didn't dare laugh. Meph-foe looked dead (pardon the expression) serious. He is really concerned about his reincarnation, as if that were possible.

"It's my religion. What's yours?"

"Music and poetry are pretty much my religion," I replied, trying to be completely honest. The truth is I don't have a religion. Most religion is mainly bullshit.

"Reincarnation. Yes, this is my prime concern, my major worry. We can come back as anything at any time in any place according to our deeds. The system is much fairer than Christianity, where you get a binary choice, heaven or hell. I could come back as a plant, maybe a giant sequoia or a form of seaweed or algae. And I could come back to a different planet. The Webb telescope shows thousands of remote galaxies, and each has 100 billion stars. Think of all the exoplanets. I want to come back here, on Earth. Earth is the right place for me. Earth is the right place for love. I can't think of any place it is likely to go better as long as I don't come back as a woman. Women get the short end of the stick, a very hard life, cooking, cleaning, shopping, washing, and little or no respect. Ugh! I could come back as a woman. That would be a severe punishment. On the other hand, I might not come back as just any woman. I might come back like some of the beauties I have known and loved or seen, divine beings like Candy Christian or Raquel Welch, or Hedy Lamarr. Did you see her film, *Ecstasy?* It's absolutely great—shows a truly beautiful woman, Hedy, at age 18, in the nude. She smokes and drinks, divorces her older husband who can't deliver, falls in love, has a wonderful orgasm, dances joyfully, and so forth. No wonder the film was one of the first to be condemned by the Legion of Decency. A film way too rich for the blood of misogynists.

"Time is also a problem. I wouldn't fit in in fourth-century Europe, for instance, nor would I fit in in the times of the dinosaurs. Ugh! I might come back in one of the other three castes: Khstsiyas (warriors), Vaishyas (merchants, landowners), Shudras (servants). Or I might come back as casteless—untouchable, suited only to clean streets, clean latrines, collect garbage. They have a bell to sound to warn the castes of their approach. They can't enter the temples. They can't read the sacred texts. This is a polluted group, filthy, polluted, unworthy. They are one-sixth of the Indian population, making 13.7% or about 120 million people. My bad karma is partly my fault but partly bad luck. Bad luck followed me like a shadow."

Meph-foe must be unhappy. Truly happy people don't pay that much attention to themselves. The unhappy take themselves very seriously!

I got up and went to the window, turning my back to Meph-foe. A rain had started streaks muttering on the pane. Oblong imperfections in the glass added to the effect of waver and blur. Squinting through the wet, I saw only scattered lights as night descended over this apprehensive city. I would eat a steak tonight and have nice strong solid drink, a vodka martini straight up with a twist of lemon but no vermouth. Hodge will be my consolation in these parlous times.

With my back to Meph, I said goodbye. I was crying and all choked up, but I managed to get some words out. "Goodbye, Meph. I am going to miss you. In my opinion, you are not so bad, and anything that might come your way should be OK."

"Wait. Let me tell you my mistakes. You decide if my karma is OK or not. Please."

"I'm no judge of anyone. I judge not, but if you feel like confessing, it is ok. I forgive everything. Confession is not needed. Go thy way and sin no more."

"Bad luck is my undoing, I tell you, not my personality or person. They kicked me out of Columbia College. The dean and several other advisors were doing the same as I was with the boy students, but I was the one who got caught and had to resign. My three marriages were failures. After seven years, Helga burst into my study and said, 'We have to talk.'"

"'About what?'"

"'This relationship, this marriage, is not working.'"

"It was like being in the movies. A B movie with B movie dialog."

"'You are boring,' she said. 'You stay in your study doing nothing but work, work, work. I can't even talk with you when I want. I'm leaving.'"

"And then she turned and left, slammed the door after her just like Nora Helmer, Torvald's wife in *A Doll's House*. She claimed her father and I had just treated her as a plaything, a doll. I ask you was that my fault? How could I help what her father did? I was just being myself and thought things were golden when, according to Helga, they weren't. The divorce was amicable. We even had a divorce party. It is like a wedding party, only better. I ask you was that my fault?

"Hard to say. Sounds like a fault on both sides."

"You bet. Helga had a man on the side, and she spent a week in Las Vegas with her podiatrist when she told me she was visiting her sister. What do you think?"

"Humm. Hard to say. Go on. But make it fast. I have to leave. Hodge is waiting."

"Wife two, Griselda, had a detective follow me and raid the motel with a photographer to take pictures of me with Rene. This was a setup because the detective said, "Good work, Rene. You know where to collect your pay."

"The third wife, Harriet, had flu and came home early and found me in bed with Billy. That was bad luck, don't you think?"

"Say no more." I waved my left hand in the air, the international sign of dismissal. "Say no more. I think you will be fortunate to come back as a dung beetle."

I turned to leave and saw that Meph-foe looked pathetic, helpless, and, for a change, silent.

* * * * *

Two weeks later, graft versus host disease set in. The docs called it GvHD. It was terrible, a terrible ordeal. The acute or fulminant form started with a rash, burning, and bright redness of the skin on palms and soles. This spread to the entire body. Nausea, vomiting, stomach cramps, severe pains, and bloody diarrhea followed. They score organ involvement 1 to 4 (gut-liver-skin). A total of 4 usually spells doom. Meph came in at a record 3-4-4, 11, a real mess. And, as predicted, he died. It seems to me the doctors use numbers to make medicine look a whole lot more scientific than it is. To me, an outsider, medicine looked like an art, a science, and, God help us, a business. What do you think?

Anyway, all the doctors and nurses agree, Meph did not ascend to heaven to the big classroom in the sky. He just lay there looking all petered out and real dead. He did not turn into a dung beetle, or a plant, or anything else but what he really was: a corpse, a very stiff, immobile corpse.

They found Clark, a pendule in Meph's office with a note pinned on his shirt: "Without him, I don't wanna live."

On his desk Meph-foe left an ENVOY:

Oh, noble women, full of high wisdom, let no humility nail down your tongues. Follow the example of Echo, who never keeps quiet but always answers back. Don't be hoodwinked in your innocence; take control into your own hands. Engrave this lesson deep in your memories, for it will work to the common profit of all mankind:

Stand up for your own rights. Don't allow men to do injustices to you. Do not fear men or their puny laws—laws made to inflict more burdens on your already over-burdened backs and souls. Be fierce as tigers. Do not let the public be the supreme judge of your lives. Be you. You wanna get high? Get high. You wanna get low? Get low. Be free to be yourselves. You know that you can.

I advise you do not fear men or pay them respect. That has been your undoing for millennia. Bind him. Make him cower like a quail. Be your female self. If you are pretty, show your face and dress in company. If you are ugly, be unusually generous. Always work hard to make friends. Be as gay in spirit as a linden leaf, and let men worry and weep, wring their hands and wail!

And so, farewell, my dearly beloveds.

Be yourselves.

And good luck to you.

Your friend, Dante

CHAPTER NINE

FORCE OF DESTINY

*"At the Resurrection, sex will be abolished, and nature made one . . .
There will then be only man as if he had never sinned."*

—Johannes Scotus Erigena

Meph's death canceled all his appointments. Death does that. After a while, the junk mail tapers off, and the phone calls eventually stop. But the debts linger on and are charged to the estate.

Dean Mary explained the course was unable to continue because they couldn't find a suitable replacement for Professor Mephistopheles, who was now professor emeritus. Tuitions were refunded, and that was that.

I talked to Ms. Weidenbaum, our school's guidance counselor, but got neither guidance nor counsel. Weid would have been better as a motivational speaker for four-year-olds on a low-budget TV children's show.

If this were a novel, we would now be at plot point one, where the narrative changes direction and aspect. But this is not a novel. This is a history, the historiography of how we women took over the world, how we settled the score. That's what it is about. At this point in my story, I assure you our mission did not change. We just had to regroup and do some serious thinking about what to do and when to do it, and especially HOW to do it.

O.K. Full disclosure: Actually, at this point, I was in bad shape. A mess. Don't get me wrong. I still had faith in the mission, but I had a desperate feeling to put something in my mouth to prevent me from screaming. Lucky, I had Hodge's shoulder to cry on. After a good hard cry, I felt much better. It's good to have memories like that filed away and good to revisit them now and then for the rest of your life.

Hodge said looking at the January 6th insurrection was a good idea. But he knew in advance why it failed. Stupid people. The people involved were stupid and disorganized, and so was Trump, who would urge them on and then tell them to go home. Leaders who do not have a clear idea of what they want are not fit to lead. Hodge said when he was Senior Patrol Leader of Boy Scout Troop 170 in Queens Village that 30 boys in the troop could have easily taken over the U.S. government because they would have been highly organized, disciplined, and much smarter than the white supremacists who failed. When I first heard this, I thought Hodge was joking, but nope, he was dead serious.

"Give me 30 stout-hearted scouts, and I will soon give you ten thousand more. Then as we, shoulder to shoulder, shoulder to shoulder, march to the fore, there is nothing in the world that can stop or mar a plan."

Follow-up on Meph's other idea about exploiting the biological differences that exist between men and women with an eye to exploiting such as weapons against men meant we needed expert advice from a biologist of mankind. And who might that be?

A physician, of course. Physicians are the foremost biologists of mankind. They have to be with all that training in college, med school, internship, residency, fellowship, and practical practice experience. We needed a physician on our team or a group of physicians. But who? Can you guess?

I pause for reply.

If you answered Hodge's father, pat yourself on the back and take a break. If you didn't answer Hodge's father, try to stay awake while you continue to read. Attention must be paid if you wish to learn important lessons. We learned our lessons the hard way. I am writing this history so you can avoid fucking up the way we almost did. You can learn the easy way by following this history, or you can fuck up. Choose!

Some people have tried to alter the facts of this history, rearrange things to suit their fancy, to tell themselves they could have done it as we did or could have done it better. There is nothing I can do about such people. They are as hopeless as the dumbbells who still think Trump won the election.

* * * * *

Doctor George Hootman, MD, FACP, FACOG, FRSM, had his women's clinic closed by Senate Bill 8 and had the IVF Institute closed after a raid that was supposed to protect embryos but resulted in massive embryo deaths when the refrigerators shut down after officers cut the power which controlled the automatic liquid nitrogen refillers.

Embryo storage tank—Over 4000 embryos in straws in that tank were lost due to the power cut. (Editor's note: Frozen embryos are kept in straws in liquid nitrogen.)

But that raid didn't stop Doctor Hootman. His clinic and the institute went underground. Funds came from his retirement monies, the sale of the 16-acre ranch in League City, a fresh mortgage on the Hootman mansion, and special donations from a former nuclear physicist and a prominent Houston socialite.

George Hootman gave it for his opinion that Senate Bill 8 would decrease the number of legal abortions, no question, but it would not decrease the number of abortions. Backalley abortion would rise, and infections and infertility, organ failure, and death would follow. We now seem destined to relearn the lessons of backalley abortion at the expense of women's lives. But wait. Why am I telling you this? I should let the doctor speak for himself. I remember most of it, and you certainly can get the gist.

First, some background according to Hodge: George majored in chemistry at Columbia College, graduated Summa Cum Laude, was elected to Alpha Omega Alpha (the nation's medical honor society) in his junior year at the College of Physicians and Surgeons, did obstetrics and gynecology residency at Johns Hopkins, was Chief Resident, then fellow in reproductive research with Landrum Shettles back at Columbia. Somewhere along the line, he served his draft obligated service as a commissioned officer in the United States Public Health Service, whatever that is. He is in good shape and recently passed his second-class aviation physical at age 81.

* * * * *

"Welcome, Lollipop. Hodge has told me about you. You are the right one for him, in my opinion. You will hold up your end of the log, and you will add intellectual interest to his life. He likes big butts and small tits, so you have the right body type for him.

"The assholes in Austin closed down my clinic and forced me underground. No way could I let women who needed my medical skill and services go wanting. In some cases, it is a matter of life or death, as you will soon see as we make rounds on the sick ladies who are here. The IVF Institute is still functioning. In fact, better than ever because other doctors are afraid of their shadows. They think having anything to do with female reproductive health will endanger their licenses, and, you know what? Those cowards are right. The trouble with doctors, in many cases, is that they went to medical school, where they learned to accept orders and salute. Consequently, in these parlous times, many doctors have lost their sangfroid and are afraid to fight. They are in a survival mode.

"At age 30, when I had a wife and two children, they drafted me into the Vietnam War. My physical shape prevented me from getting through basic training alive, so they exempted me and assigned me to the U.S. Public Health Service."

Me: "Public Health Service? What's that?"

"Don't feel bad. Most people know nothing about it. It is the brain-child of Frances Perkins, the Secretary of Labor under FDR, and a very remarkable and very unique woman. No—that's incorrect usage. A woman is unique or not unique and can't be very unique because unique means, well, unique, one of a kind.

"Frances came up with two other progressive ideas: Social Security and Unemployment Insurance. FDR got most of the credit for these wonderful social reforms, but the basic ideas came from Frances. Nurturing ideas and social protective nets and networks are typical female things, and that is why they came from a woman.

"Frances was the first female member of a presidential cabinet and became the longest-serving member of that cabinet. Her vision was that there should be a corps of officers, somewhat like in the military, whose job was to preserve and protect the public health by making war on disease. In my oath for my commission as a commander, I swore to uphold the constitution and to obey all lawful and reasonable orders. This is the same oath taken by military officers. Get it? There is no obligation to obey an unreasonable order. If that is good enough for the American military, then it is good enough for me in dealing with laws handed down by the assholes in the Texas Senate.

"Ready for rounds?"

We entered a room that looked like Meph's room at M.D. Anderson, only bigger, but no windows because we were in a basement. This was also rotunda style, with the nurses' station in the center and the patient rooms radiating. Three nurses were on duty.

Slogans posted on the walls read:

FREEDOM TO CHOOSE

EVERY BABY A WANTED BABY

TAKE BACK THE NIGHT

LET THERE BE NO BOUNDARIES

NO CONTINGENCIES

A WOMAN'S PLACE IS IN THE HOUSE AND SENATE

RECAPTURE OUR BODIES

A WOMAN'S PLACE IS NOT ON THE KITCHEN TABLE

Under that slogan, the picture of a woman's body on a table with blood dripping out of her you-know-what.

SENATE BILL 8 STINKS

The next sign would be considered blasphemy by some religious nuts, but I see it as a joke:

IN GOD WE TRUST. ALL OTHERS PAY CASH

George said he pays the nurses well in cash, but he has not paid himself a dime in the last three months since he set things up. Hodge had to give up his allowance. "I'm part of the great American middle-class middle class again and getting used to it. Hodge is part of the riffraff lower classes and getting used to it."

George introduced the first patient, who was a 22-year-old mother of two. She was six months pregnant.

"Martha is pregnant with twins. Notice her belly is like a huge melon. Humungous. I would like to call your attention to this tissue on the right side of her forehead. What do you make of it?"

On her forehead was a curious fleshy extension that looked like a miniature human leg with a small foot that had three toes. Martha, with sad, tired eyes, said I may touch it, and I did. It was flesh and warm and withdrew a little with my touch. Whatever it was, it seemed alive, and I assumed it was part of Martha or something embedded in her skull, now poking out into the air. Some kind of parasite? Or maybe a tumor. Nothing good. I turned to George and said, "I give up. It might be a parasite. I can't make heads or tails of it."

George said, "It is neither a head nor a tail. It's a leg. It's the other twin. One twin is in the oven, the uterus. The other twin is growing in mom's head. This is an ectopic pregnancy. The embryo got in the wrong place probably via abnormal circulation of blood from the placenta into the general maternal blood stream resulting in a freak of nature. A big problem for mom as it is also putting pressure on her brain. Should I call the assholes in Austin and ask what to do? They would tell me to keep my hands in my pocket and do nothing. That's the law. Do nothing at present. When the condition results in an emergency and mom's life is in danger, then you may intervene. That's the way this kooky law is written. No kidding. Completely absurd!

"Mom's twin baby in the uterus and the other twin, the monster in mom's skull bone, and mom herself will then all three die—die after lots of pain and suffering. This ectopic pregnancy is unusual. Usually, they end up in the fallopian tube or attached to the colon or perineum. I had one woman with one in the liver. Moles are closely related."

Me: "Moles?"

"Another freak of nature. God must have a cosmic sense of humor to make these freaks and throw them at us.

"Sometimes two sperms enter the same egg. That gives the embryo 96 chromosomes, two from dad and one set from mom (23 + 23 + 23 = 96). The trophoblast continues to grow, making a mess. Removal of the mess saves the mother's life. Sometimes the trophoblast continues growing, creating a gestational trophoblastic neoplasm which can lead to metastatic choriocarcinoma. But that is a relatively easy cancer to cure because it has paternal antigens that mom's immune system will attack in addition to the chemotherapy we give. Am I snowing you? Too much information?"

Me: "Not at all. Very interesting and very complicated. You're joking about consulting the Texas senators. They probably don't know beans about this stuff."

"Tomorrow, two volunteer plastic surgeons and I will work six to eight hours removing this monster from Martha's head. At the end of the day, her head will look pretty good, and six weeks from now, it will look pretty normal.

"To Martha and to her husband, we doctors will be heroes. To the state of Texas, we'll be criminals. But you know what, I don't give a fuck. Premium non nocere—first do no harm. Saving lives is what I like to do and will do until I can't do it anymore. Besides, they have to catch me first, and, also, I don't think any jury will convict me of any crime for saving a mother's life."

At this point, George smiled, took a deep breath, puffed out his chest, and started singing:

"Every man has a job to do

And my job is doing good.

Every night when the job is through

I hang up my coat

Proud to know I've done what I could.

Oh, it's a satisfying feeling when you turn in late

To know you've averted the diseases people hate

Every man has a job to do

And my job is doing good

Oh, I'll never stop,

Never stop,

Doing good!"

Rounds continued. The next patient had placenta privia, a condition where the placenta, instead of placing itself on the top or side of the uterus, landed on the cervix, obstructing the birth canal. No doubt the assholes in Austin wouldn't know what placenta privia was, much less what to do about it.

News Flash: NBC News: Kansas recount confirms results in favor of abortion rights. The attempt to limit abortion rights failed by 18% or 165,000 votes statewide. Fewer than 100 votes were changed by the recount. The republicans paid $120,000 for the recount and now agree the results are correct. GOP activists recognize what they call a dark era of life in the state where women have human rights. One pundit who had lived in the state his whole life said, "I no longer recognize my Kansas. This is the beginning. Soon women will be permitted to marry who they want, wear what they want, eat what they want. If this nightmare can happen in Kansas, it can happen anywhere. The big mistake was giving women the right to vote. It is too late to change that for this election. But we can try for the next."

Nurses and patients were screaming and jumping up and down, hugging each other. I was screaming too. But then I saw it and stopped. Hodge and George were crying. Actually crying. I hate to see grown men cry. They were crying for the joy of it, the way we women sometimes cry after a good orgasm. When George got control of himself, he said, "Wow! There's hope. We have to celebrate at lunch. A great day for women's rights! Wonderful news!

The next patient had an even more complicated condition with the chorion, and the amnion separated when they should have fused. This freak of nature causes plenty of problems for fetus and mother. The amnion is a membrane-like plastic wrap. The chorion is a membrane-like wax paper. George explained what he was going to do to ameliorate the situation, but I forgot what he said. It was clear to me that the jerks in the legislature had no business making laws controlling medical procedures or preventing doctors like George from doing their thing.

George checked his Apple watch and announced that it was lunchtime. "Let's go to Le Jardinier at the Museum of Fine Arts Houston. The chef, Alain, had one Michelin star before coming here. His is the best restaurant in Houston. Real high class and expensive, but great. We need to patronize it while it is still in business. Most of the really great restaurants can't make it for long. Not enough people appreciate truly great dining. Let's celebrate the Kansas result. What say?"

* * * * *

Le Jardinier is in the new Nancy and Rich Kinder building on the west side of the MFAH. It is bright, modern, and spacious, with a full bar and a cathedral ceiling. We sat at a table for four in the center of the dining room. The bar along the eastern wall looked quite well-equipped with adult beverages. I had my usual Sky vodka martini straight up with a twist of lemon and no vermouth, and Hodge had his usual Jameson Irish whiskey on the rocks, a double. George had water because he said he had D&Cs scheduled that afternoon. He held his glass of water on high and offered a toast: "Here's to the D&C. What would we do without the D&C?

"There are three D&Cs scheduled for this afternoon. All these ladies have well-established families, and they don't want another child. I will save them and help their finances, their educational opportunities, their mental health, their jobs, and their happy relationship with their husbands. The Brookings Institute just released the data on the cost of raising a child to age 17. For a married middle-class family with two children already, the third child will cost $310,605 total or $18,221 a year.

"Patient four has a difficult choice to make and has not decided what to do. She is pregnant with child number three and says she wants a third child. She loves babies. But she also has a very malignant intraductal adenocarcinoma of the breast. The usual treatment would be surgery, radiation, and chemotherapy with a very high rate of cure. But the chemo will hurt her and the fetus. In addition, there is the option of newer, much more effective, and truly life-saving treatments based on a keen understanding of the physiology of the cancer cell. Those newer treatments hit cell surface markers on the cancer cell and destroy the cancer, but all of them are contraindicated in pregnancy because they almost always produce fetal deformity or death. In the old days, women in her shoes had the option of selecting the treatment they felt was in their best interest. As her doctor, my job is to tell her the facts and help her as much as I can, but the decision what to do is hers and should be hers. Right now, here in Texas, that decision has been made by Senate bill 8, and one major option for her life and treatment has been taken away from her.

"Shared decision-making is a cornerstone of medical practice. Physicians routinely work with patients to balance their beliefs and values with their therapeutic options. Weighing risks and benefits of de-escalation of systemic therapy (in other words cutting down on the poisons and the more effective treatments), the interplay between these choices and surgery and radiation, and the effects of treatments on the survival of the patient and the health of the fetus defies the blunt instrument of legal regulations that antiabortion forces have now forced on Texas women.

"We physicians have an obligation to advocate for our patients. New restrictions on reproductive choices have a gigantic adverse effect on medical care, and doctors should be screaming to protect patients who could become or who are pregnant. Why are they not screaming? I'll tell you why: They are cowards!

"D&C is quick, effective, and safe. If she wants it, she shall have it. The law is wrong from the start. Stupidity has to stop."

Editor's note: D&C is medical talk for dilation and curettage where the cervix is dilated and the inner part of the uterus, the uterine lining, is surgically cleared and cleaned. Blood clots, infected tissue, tumors, and the products of conception can be removed safely and effectively.

* * * * *

We three all ate the grilled octopus that came with smoked fingerling potatoes, tasso, and paprika aioli, and for the main course, we ate the arctic char that came with heirloom squash, tomato, and pistachio gremolata. Nothing like it—truly delicious and very good for us but not so good for the octopus and the char.

Dessert for Hodge and George was the butterfly, delicate yuzu mousse, raspberry compote, and sorbet. This was a work of art. If I find a picture, I will paste it in. The butterfly is edible candy. Yummy!

My dessert was plant-based ice cream. I thought I would try it to see if it was the same as the real thing made from dairy. The chocolate plant ice cream was excellent, so good I have serious questions as to whether it was actually plant-based. If it is, it is a miracle.

The Butterfly Dessert

That D&C toast reminded George of his fellowship with Landrum Shettles, MD, Ph.D. at Columbia. His story was quite interesting, and I'll let him tell it the way he told it to us at lunch:

"Landrum was my mentor, a genius way ahead of his time and most times right. He was associate professor at the College of Physicians and Surgeons Columbia University and had a laboratory in Presbyterian Hospital where he did scientific work on how human eggs are fertilized and how and when they are implanted in the uterus lining. His book, *Ovum Humanum*, with beautiful color pictures of human eggs in various stages of development, is a classic. He worked closely with John Rock at Harvard until John dropped out of the research because of adverse peer pressure. Anything that deals with human reproduction spooks administrators and committees and legislators and religious nuts. George Pincus, who was working with Rock at Harvard, got fired. That was the handwriting on the wall for Rock, who then devoted his time to research on a special new thing—what was it?"

Me: "The pill."

"Right. Rock's pill research was sponsored by Margaret Sanger, who saw it as a liberating item much needed by women.

"Landrum was also censored by Columbia Faculty, particularly by Raymond Vand Wiele, the chairman of the department of obstetrics and gynecology, because of 'odd work habits.' In 1960 and 1962, Landrum actually achieved invitro fertilization, the production of a fertilized human egg outside of the human body. The pictures are amazing, showing the rather large egg surrounded by the little tadpole-like sperms trying to enter. When one got in, the egg membrane suddenly blocked the other sperms from entering. One time out of a thousand, two sperms might get in, creating a non-viable embryo and a defective fetus with the wrong number of chromosomes or the wrong type of chromosomes, or both.

"Landrum also invented injecting sperm directly into fallopian tubes, sometimes correcting infertility by bypassing the vagina. This did not go well with the department chair nor with the human experiment committee, but the infertile couples who got babies loved it.

"The crisis came in 1975 when a surgeon at the New York Hospital, Sweeney—I think was his name, yes William Sweeney asked Landrum about bypassing the fallopian tubes completely in a woman, Doris Del-Zio, whose tubes had been scarred by infection.

"Sweeney removed eggs from the woman's ovary, and her husband, John, who was also a doctor, rushed the eggs across town in a taxi to Landrum's lab. Doctor John then supplied sperm, and bingo—a human embryo was created in a test tube. No embryo can implant in the uterus until days five to seven of life. So, Landrum was keeping this new human, the proud parents' daughter (chromosome counts had been done, and the baby was XX), in tissue culture supplying the necessary nutrients.

"Raymond Vand Wiele, the chairman, asked to see the experiment and cruelly unstoppered the tube ending the experiment and killing the embryo. Thus, Columbia University lost the chance of becoming the world leader in fertility medicine.

"Much trouble followed. Landrum was fired even though he had tenure, and his lab was wrecked and all embryos destroyed. Landrum left Columbia and, after a brief stay in New York City as director of the New York Fertility Foundation, moved to Vermont as chief of Obstetrics and Gynecology at Gillford Memorial Hospital in Randolph, Vermont, where he continued to do research, this time on clones, asexual reproduction of cells identical to the ancestor. He had suffered enough trying to do fertility research and had thrown in the towel.

"Of course, that wasn't the end of it. The parents, the Del-Zios, in the true American tradition, sued the university for 1.5 million dollars and collected, according to court records, $50,000. Rumor has it Landrum sued, and the university settled for three million dollars, plus restoration of Landrum's title. But we are not sure of all that because those records are sealed."

Note from me (Lollipop): I here attach a picture of the egg surrounded by sperms. Biology is amazing. The article I read said Landrum discovered that male sperms (Y) swim faster and live shorter than female sperms (X). Therefore, Landrum said if you have intercourse three days before ovulation, the chance of getting a girl is increased as the X sperms survive longer to get to the egg. If you have intercourse on the day of ovulation, the chance of getting a boy is increased because the Y sperms swim faster to get to the egg. He also suggested vinegar douche if you want a girl and that the woman not have an orgasm during sex if you want a girl. Subsequent studies showed the technique, now known as the *Shettles Method*, is about 75% effective.

Our own method, developed by Usha, completely separates Y sperms out and leaves only X sperms. Our method is 100% effective in producing females and only females. This was an important technical advance enabling us women to populate the planet with women and only women.

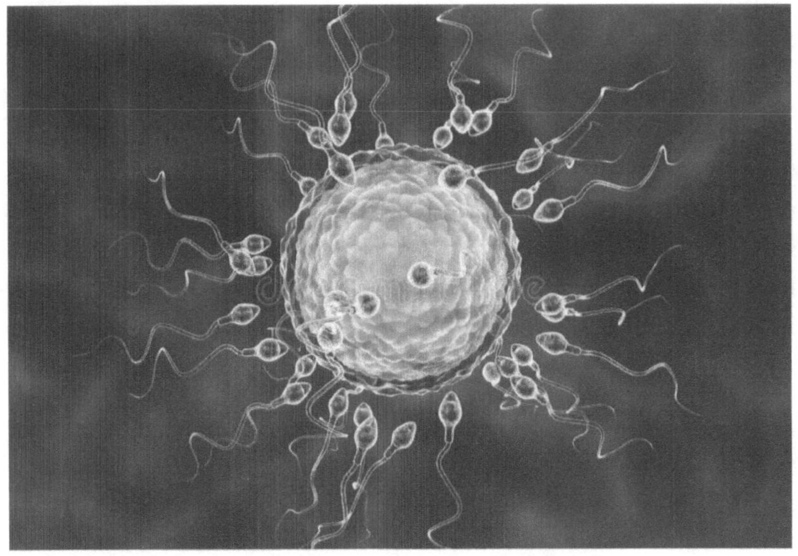

Egg surrounded by eager sperms

* * * * *

After lunch, Hodge drove us home to the RV park. I napped on the way but was shaken awake when we turned left and headed east on Miles Road.

"Hodge, your father didn't say what he did during the war."

"That's right."

"What's right?"

"He didn't say what he did."

"Hodge, will you cut it out. What did he do?"

"During his draft obligated service, he worked for the government."

"Obviously. But doing what?"

"Lollipop, dad doesn't like to talk about it, and neither do I. He refused to wear a uniform and wouldn't let them cut his hair. He told his captain, I don't want to be here. The government is forcing me. I won't wear a uniform, so you can put me in the brig for two years, and I will serve out my time reading novels. Or you can let me take care of these poor slobs who think they have been fighting for their country. Choose!

"Dad took care of a floor of inpatients at the National Institutes of Health Hospital in building 10, did medical consults there, and at the National Naval Medical Center Hospital across the street and at Walter Reed down the road. They gave him a laboratory in the basement and a wonderful technician (Catherine Oliver), lots of money, equipment, two rooms full of monkey cages filled with monkeys, one room of mice and rats, also in cages, and an office with bookcases, a desk, and a telephone.

"One of his clinical jobs was to take care of the United States Senators. He was at the beck and call of the senate. He often had lunch in the senate dining room, usually with Taft of Ohio and Prince of Maryland. Senate dining room—cost nine million dollars, labor not included. Each table of four has two waiters. The women who bring the drinks are so stacked they can balance the cocktails on their tits. Along the sides are the nap rooms which senators can also use for private time with a page or intern, or secretary.

"Dad's research job was to study neuromuscular transmission."

"What's that?" I asked as Hodge unlocked the three locks on the door to the camper and stepped inside.

Hodge opened the refrig and got himself a coke. He chugged and wiped his mouth with his sleeve. "The nerve tells the muscle when and how much to contract by sending an electric impulse to the end of the nerve where the muscle is. The nerve releases a chemical called acetylcholine, and this chemical travels across the gap between nerve and muscle to hit a receptor on the muscle. The receptor then reacts and causes the muscle to contract. An enzyme, acetylcholine esterase, stops the process and relaxes the muscle.

"It took me 27 seconds to tell you that, but it took 27 years for scientists to figure it out. The place where nerve meets muscle is called the neuromuscular junction. Pretty cool, right?"

That is one of the endearing features about Hodge: He knows lots about useless things. But once he gets started, it is hard for him to shut up and zip it. Thus, he continued.

"The neuromuscular junction is the center of several diseases including myasthenia gravis, puffer fish poisoning, antibiotic-induced muscle weakness, blue-rimmed octopus bite, and it is the center of effect of nerve gases, one of the centers. There are lots of places in the human body where acetylcholine causes something to happen—sweating, gut motility, pupillary contraction, heart action, and so forth.

He: "Are we going to screw tonight?"

Me: "That depends. Right now, I'm not in the mood."

He: "Can you get in the mood?"

Me: "Hard to say. I am excessively moody, probably that time of the month."

He: "That's fine. I'm a good soldier."

Me: "Meaning what?"

He: "I'm not afraid of getting my sword bloody."

Me: "Ha ha. Some floozy told you that."

He: "Lynn and I were a pair for a while until she fell madly in love with a civil engineer who happened to be black. The marriage didn't last long. He was an intrepid gambler and managed to engineer the loss of all his assets and hers. They wound up throwing the keys to their heavily mortgaged home in Kingswood on the kitchen table and walking. Not good for the credit ratings, but hell, they were stuck. The story doesn't end there: Monsieur had sex with Lynn's daughter (from a previous marriage). Whether this was incest or lust depends on the definition. I think it was more likely lust. The engineer and the daughter were not biologically related. There followed the birth of a mixed-race boy whom Lynn loved. No change that. Loved is not the word. Lynn adored her grandson. Still does."

Me: "Nerve gases? Wasn't that what Saddam Insane was going to use? Some powerful instrument of mass destruction."

"Hah! His name was Saddam Hussein. And yes, he said he had nerve gases, but none were found after we liberated Iraq. He was bluffing, or maybe he destroyed them. Who knows. By the way, there are no such things as nerve gases. They are not gases at all. They are dispersible liquids, including VX, ten milligrams of which can kill a man in minutes. Dad worked two years trying to find an antidote to VX and VX2 and saran and the other organophosphates, and then one day, he was sitting in the library of the National Institutes of Health reading an interesting article about how people treated with chemotherapy lost their hair and then regrew it darker, thicker, and curlier than it had been before, when suddenly, like a bolt of lightning out of the blue the answer came to him. It was one of those ah-ha moments like Kercule dreaming about the structure of benzene by seeing a snake bite its tail. The structure of C6H6 was a ring! It was like Archimedes shouting eureka as he discovered the law of displacement as he hopped into his bath.

"The answer was *block the receptor*, and dad knew how to do it. He rushed to the lab, had Catherine set up the experiment, and bingo. All the animals injected with the blocker survived VX as if nothing happened. All the others not so treated died.

"Dad got promoted to Rear Admiral, one star, got a raise, and was paid $8,600 reward for the discovery and an additional $8,600 incentive pay to stay in service six more months to perfect the work. Dad was not happy with the implications. Now American troops could use VX with impunity on an enemy not protected. Dad was assured the American army would never ever use VX against humans. It might use it as an exclusionary device. Put the stuff in an area you don't want others to enter. It is like a land mine. Only it doesn't explode. It is pretty much nonvolatile and will only kill those who enter the exposed area."

"Hodge, I am feeling sad about Meph-foe and the course, and sad about your father, who deserves better treatment, and sad about what is happening to women's rights and all that. I need some hugs and pets. How about we just hug and that's all. Hugs—that's what I need. OK?"

"OK, but first you have to answer a question, an important question. Lollipop, do you love me?"

"I'm not sure."

"Lollipop, that was not the answer I was looking for, but I guess it will do for the moment. Let's hit the sack and hug. I am not feeling so great myself. The times are out of joint. Oh, wretched spite that we were ever born to set things right."

* * * * *

Cramps woke me at midnight. I stanched the flow with a tampon from my purse. While having a nice relaxing pee in Hodge's claustrophobic cramped closet toilet, I looked at my multiple images reflected in the two mirrors. I extended to infinity north and south and got smaller as the distance increases but was still me. I smiled, and I smiled back. I waved, and ditto. The illusion taught me that I could seem like many more people than I was. I could look extended much farther than I really did.

I lectured my multiple mirror images. "Andzelika Dziedzic, time to convert anger to action. You have a date with destiny. Men have abused power and have abused women way too much and for too long. It has to stop. Most Americans agree. A vocal minority has had a say far beyond their numbers. They must be deposed. We have reached the tipping or the tripping point. Whatever. We must take up arms against a sea of troubles and, by opposing, end them. What we need is a team of rough, tough women used to working as a group, not afraid of getting hurt. They must have a clear unshakable image of the mission and its importance. Men are basically cowards. Look at what happened at Uvalde: 376 men armed to the teeth with a SWAT team, automatic weapons, and bulletproof shields—and yet they were afraid to go in and take out the lone shooter. The cops were afraid they might get hurt. Mrs. Gomez broke loose, jumped the fence, entered through a window, and rescued her two children and others. How's that for pussy power! Those heavily armed men were cowards. From which follows:

We might. We just might intimidate men into surrendering. The best battles are won by not toeing the line. This would be a truly feminine way of taking over, taking over without force or violence. And then controlling things with charm. That was the hope, anyway. So, we needed a team of women who could instill fear into the hearts of men and make men give up, lay down their weapons, and play nice with others. We needed women strong enough, powerful enough, fast enough, and determined enough to instill the fear of God into men. We needed women willing to rebut and extinguish the constraints placed on them by a patristic society.

Where would I find such ladies? I knew exactly where to look. And readers, those of you paying attention and thinking, also know. Where else would we find tough babes and bitches eager to fight and fully capable of fighting, fighting for a just cause? Where else would we find such ladies but at—ROLLER DERBY!"

CHAPTER TEN

ROLLER DERBY—IT'S NOT JUST ROLLER SKATING

"A woman needs a man as much as a fish needs a bicycle."

—Gloria Steinem

Roller derby—I don't know much about it. Roller skating—I don't know much about it either, but I did do some in my salad days on those metal skates that needed a key to lock the skates on your feet. And I fell on my ass more times than I remember. I had so many bruises on my legs and knees my mother took me to the doctor to see if I had leukemia. Nope, no leukemia. Just too many falls.

Roller derby is a unique stage for women via costumes, derby names, and derby personas. Arafat gave the opinion, "Roller derby defies heteronormality and patriarchal standards. In Egypt, women do not exhibit visible scars, (they) refrain from activities that may damage their bodies, and (they) keep their bodies unblemished and perfect for their husbands. In Egypt, roller derby is subversive as it acts as a political statement." And that, friends, is why roller derby is forbidden by law in so many countries.

Hot dog! If Arafat speaks true, roller derby will supply just the kind of women we need for our mission.

Most of what I know about roller derby comes from my friend, Cherry Bomb, who lives it, and from the times my mom told me about how she watched banked curved track roller derby on a 9-inch Dumont TV in 1948. Yes, I have seen a few flat tract events myself, about 15, but I had trouble following who was doing what and why. Reading Shauna Cross's book *Whip It* helps, and so does the movie by the same name starring Ellen Page.

I guess you know in December 2021, Canadian actress Ellen Page announced she was transgender, identifies as male, and wants henceforth to be called Elliot Page. In 2018, she/he married a woman, Emma Portner. They divorced in 2021. Elliot is a woke person. More power to him! I hope he is happy now. He told the media he felt he was a boy from age nine onward and now was what he had always been and wanted to be.

To me, Ellen/Elliot look good each in her/his way. What do you think?

Ellen at left. Elliot at right.

Doctor Hootman says the Page story is not unusual. Human sexuality and gender identification are quite complicated. Usually, in the development of the fetus, the female brain matches up with a female body, and a male brain matches with a male body. But occasionally, they don't match, and a female is born with a male brain and vice versa. Doctor Hootman told us about one of his patients who, at age 10, went to her room and tried to cut off her tits with a scissor leading to a bloody mess. She was sure she was a boy and had been given the wrong body. Modern science supports her view and says she is right. She has a brain-body mismatch, the basic cause of gender dysphoria.

Since current technology can't change the brain, therapy must be directed to changing the body. Doctors try to get things as close to the natural condition as they can. They try but often don't quite make it. It is interesting to note, says Doctor Hootman, that there are distinct differences between the male and female brains. Male brains are larger, for instance. Even more important is the anatomic distribution and size of different brain regions, male versus female. For instance, the corpus callosum is larger in females suggesting interhemispheric communication is greater in females than in males. The magnetic resonance scans show distinct differences in processing. People have the processing signals of the gender they identify with rather than their body type. Thus, a person with a female body like Elliot, who says she is a male, would actually be predicted to have a male pattern of brain function. Fascinating! Right! And proof that the transgender kids are in need of sympathy and medical help. Current laws in many states don't recognize the biological facts here and tend to impose a non-scientific and even criminal view on being trans. The American Medical Association has condemned those states and those laws to no avail.

And guess what? People who identify as neither male nor female, who think they are in between sexes, have a mixed in-between Magnetic Image scan. They, therefore, probably have a brain that is about half female and half male.

The scientific study of sex is in its infancy. Too bad the congress cut off all federal grants to study human sexuality. No kidding. Professor Elain Hull, chair of the Department of Biology at Tallahassee, told me her grant to study homosexual rats was terminated by the legislation that stopped all federal support of sex research. Elain never explained how she found homosexual rats. Unlikely that they frequented gay bars. Actually, she isolated a brain protein that controlled expression of homosexuality in the rats, but she was unable to follow up on her discovery because the congress cut her research grant.

The congress also cut off all federal funds to study gun violence. I guess they figure what they don't know won't hurt them. No change that. The congress probably knows what scientists find out about sex and about gun violence will hurt them by offending their stupid ultra-religious and ultra-conservative voting base they need for reelection. Sex research and gun violence research still go on, but only if supported by funds from private donors.

* * * * *

Where was I? Oh, yea, Cherry Bomb. She stands five-foot-ten in her stocking feet, has jet black hair cut short but with spikes. She says, "The shorter the hair, the closer to God." I have not figured what she meant by that, and I didn't ask. Black big malignant eyebrows and overly bright red lipstick make her look kinda goth, like a character in the movie *Rocky Horror Picture Show* with the same androgyny that widened the sphere for gender expression. Lots of eye shadow. In roller derby, you can't get enough eye shadow. Plenty of tattoos adorn her body, most covered by clothes. The ones I have seen include two multicolored birds on her ankles, a large black arrow on the inner aspect of her left thigh points to her crotch. On top, the arrow in bold red letters read: "This way to bliss." On the back of her neck extending down the midsection of her back appears a beautiful multicolored angel (reds, blues, yellows, and greens mainly), a birthday gift from her girlfriend, Mary Merciless, or is it Merciless Mary? Lots of derby kisses, of course. Derby kisses—that's derby slang for black and blue bruises—they come with the sport.

Cherry Bomb used to call herself Wild Cherry. She said that was OK for night club work at Gilley's, but Cherry Bomb fit better the alter ego she assumes when she skates in competition.

Cherry Bomb spent her preteen years counting down to the freedom that would come with a driver's license. She managed to graduate high school and actually has an MBA from University of Houston. She worked for various organizations (hospitals mainly) but ended up fired for various reasons, including doing lines of coke in the laundry room or sitting in her office with a loaded Smith & Wesson Airweight revolver in her mouth.

Diagnosed finally as bipolar and put on proper treatment (she swallows a cupful of pills each morning) has made her look, feel, and be fairly normal for a goth dork. There are no insane people, in my opinion, only sick ones who need help.

VD? You bet. She has had her share. The herpes is persistent, and she takes a pill every day to keep it under control. When it flares, she takes two pills. Twelve-step? You bet. Her drinks are margaritas and Lone Star beer. Her favorite song: *Regrette Rien* by Edith Piaf.

You get the picture. Need I say more?

Cherry Bomb's mom is a construction worker. Dad was a fighter pilot killed in World War II. Consequently, there are no property taxes on the little rundown cottage they live in in Pasadena, Texas. Harris county exempts your property if you get killed in battle. Also, you get four whole months of combat pay and a nice aluminum coffin draped with an American flag with a two-nurse honor guard accompanying you home in the Hercules Cargo Master. All that just for getting killed. The lucky stiffs!

Strange how the mind works. It just crossed my mind wondering if Meph-foe ever saw a roller derby. I miss him and hope he came back as something good.

Pasadena held a roller derby at the Pasadena Convention Center and Municipal Fairgrounds, 7902 Fairmont Parkway, Pasadena, Texas. Cherry Bomb was hooked at first sight and went up and volunteered as fresh meat. (Fresh meat is derby talk meaning a new recruit,) Her ice-skating experience helped, and after hundreds of falls, bruises, sprains, two torn ligaments, and a broken toe, she was on the team.

We, you and I, dear reader, are about to talk with Cherry Bomb when we will drop in during practice at the Pearland Southside Roller Derby, Pearworld Skate Center, 1230 Broadway, Pearland. Roller Derby stopped in Houston because of the pandemic and has not yet restarted. But the ladies still meet to keep up skills. The adult meeting is Wednesday 7:00 - 8:30 PM.

Let's visit with the Houston Roller Derby crowd. But before the visit, we should bone up on roller derby. I think we should have some background info so we look reasonably in the swim. I didn't know this stuff, so I looked it up on Wiki. Knowledge is power. I wanted to look like I knew something about roller derby as I was going to ask the roller ladies to help with the avulsion. Makes sense, right? Be prepared!

General Patton said time spent in reconnaissance is never wasted. Here's what I learned:

Houston Roller Derby started in 2004 as Space City Rollergirls, Inc. Subsequently, the skaters took over, and the corporation is now skater owned and operated as a democracy with elected officers and decisions by committees. Along the line, on March 11, 2011, they became a public charity known as Houston Rollergirls, Inc. and doing business as Houston Roller Derby. This a key point in our story because, as a 501(c)(3) tax-exempt non-profit, we were able to funnel money to them, and the donors got a tax deduction. Our original intention was that they (Rollergirls) could distribute the funds which we intended to use to buy weapons, mainly semiautomatics like AK-47, 45 caliber Uzis, and Calicos (with the cylindrical magazine that holds 100 bullets), navy concussion grenades, and some smoke bombs—just enough to scare men to surrender as was our plan. Claudia wised us up, and the plans for weapons changed to something better and much more effective, as you will see if you keep reading.

Money donated to roller derby was also diverted for biological research, which came up with our super cool virus weapon that kills the human Y chromosome (to be explained later), and money for the vaccines we needed to save the lives of the men who had helped us win freedom. Without money in America, you can't wiggle. Without money, you can't do medical research. Without money, it is hard to do anything.

Real cool, right! We thought we would use the tax system invented and controlled by men to outfit our avulsion. We thought we would use the failure of congress to outlaw weapons and chemicals to arm our women and train them.

But now, for the sake of better public relations, the avulsion is called *The Unpleasantness*, sort of like the Irish calling the 30-year war about the status of Northern Ireland *The Troubles*.

* * * * *

The meeting took place on August 25, 2022, a day that will live in infamy. A day that the law in Texas forbidding abortion went into full effect, a law that makes no exceptions for rape or incest. I kid you not! And a recent survey by Beto's team (Beto is running for governor against Abbott) showed 82% of Texans favor legal abortion. So why the disconnect between the will of the people and the law? Simple, in fact, expected. The men in the legislature obviously do not truly represent the people of this state. They definitely don't represent the women.

* * * * *

Cherry Bomb spotted me right away.

"Hey, Lollipop, you here, bitch. You fresh meat?"

"Ha, some joke, I have neither the body type nor the mental armor to do roller derby, but I would like to talk to you in private."

"What? I thought you straight."

"Very straight. But this is about a very important matter. More important than sex. Please, you know I'm your fan, the president, in fact, of your fan club."

"Lollipop, kissing ass is not going to get you on my team. I know my fan club has only one person—you."

Cherry Bomb cupped her mouth and shouted to the group waiting. "Lollipop here is my fan. It's about time I had a fan. She and I need to talk."

We huddled in a corner away from Razor Blade, the male coach, and out of hearing of the others.

Cherry Bomb said, "Make it fast. There are only seven more minutes to water break."

I explained everything at the speed of light. She was all in.

Cherry: "Damn! That's great. About time women took the reins and beat the horses. Let me talk to the others. Everything on the QT. No social media. Messages only and them erased after received. This has to be a surprise—a big surprise. But without moola, we no can do. Nada, amiga. Get the dough, and you get us. Without bread, we can't do nothing. Believe it or not, we are a public charity, one of those 501 things. Tonight, I will send a list of names. There are 1250 leagues worldwide, all amateur, self-organized, all democratic, and all female. Plenty of women hot to go to bat for the cause. Recruiting outside Houston will take time, but not much. We know how to network. It's in our blood."

The whistle blew. "Gotta go, bitch. Stay for the jam. Will you?"

To practice and strategize, the Psych Ward Sirens were divided into two teams of five each for the jam. Each team of five selected a jammer who got the helmet with the white star on it. The other four members of the team were blockers. The whistle blew, and seconds later, two ladies had already hit the floor and were moaning. Seconds later, another whistle and the jammers took off, and a third skater fell, and another had been pushed or skated out of bounds. Skaters leaped over the fallen to block the jammer and promptly fell on their asses. One of the skaters couldn't get up. Play stopped, and EMS put her on a stretcher, and she disappeared out the door. I left with her because I didn't want to see any more mayhem. When they tell us roller derby is a contact sport, that is an understatement.

The Psych Ward Sirens mean business. If I can find it, I will attach their logo, which is part of the punk aesthetic.

That evening I got the list from Cherry Bomb. The pseudonyms—the derby names that are taken very seriously. They are satirical, mock-violent, sexual puns, and alliterate allusions to popular culture. Names that reflect as Cherry Bomb told us the alternate egos they adopt while skating. Even roller derby events have unusually catchy names like Spanksgiving, Seasons Beatings, Cinco de Mayhem, and War of the Wheels.

Here is the original list of our women heroes. After *The Unpleasantness*, their names will be inscribed on a gigantic white marble structure on the mall in Washington, D.C., right next to the Vietnam War Memorial, which has 58,000 names to our 25. The Vietnam names are those of the dead. Because of careful planning, none of our heroes died. Death is a man thing. Life is a woman thing. Never the two shall meet until men and women stand face to face before God's great judgment seat.

The names are in no particular order. Cherry Bomb said they elected Malice in Wonderland the leader. Cherry assured me they are all misfits, with not a single mainstream woman among them, but all are kind, and they are all all-in with the program.

1. Malice in Wonderland

2. Allegra Gaiter

3. Betty Machete

4. Diana Demon

5. Juana Beatem

6. Eva Destruction

7. Baby Ruthless

8. Tinker Hell

9. Vera Vulture

10. Diana Might

11. Annie Social

12. Kami Kazzi

13. Martha Mayhem

14. Black Widow

15. Sandra Sandbag

16. Emma Geddon

17. Crystal Death

18. Wendy Whipper

19. Bonnie Blackjack

20. VD Vera

21. Hurl Scout

22. Mary Merciless

23. Jekyll and Heidi

24. Cherry Bomb

25. Iron Maiden

P.S. The names, cool monikers, are on loan to you by the girls who really skate them. The whistle just blew. Got to line up for time trials. More later, maybe. Cherry.

That's great. All the personnel are lined up like ducks in a row.

Willie Sutton, famous bank robber, when asked why he robs banks, famously replied, "That's where the money is."

Now we needed to get money. I know where to start. I know where the money is.

Do you?

CHAPTER ELEVEN

MONEY AND A CHANGE IN DIRECTION

"The absurd man is he who never changes."

—Camus

Yesterday, August 26, 2022, was National Women's Equality Day, commemorating the certification of the 19th amendment on August 26, 1920. Window dressing of little significance. Here we are over 100 years later with women's rights under serious attack. We, women, are no longer interested in equality. No sir. We want inequality, with women controlling everything and men controlling nothing.

Alert readers guessed that I would head today to the baseball diamond on Highway 3 in Webster, Texas, to try to talk Claudia Couvert out of her money. Before going, I first made a mission statement in case she asked for one. Mission statements are the current rage among corporations, schools, churches, newspapers, TV stations, political parties, and what have you. They mostly are bullshit—things done for show without due regard to the truth. Our mission is clear and was first articulated by the wife of Bath in *Chaucer's Canterbury Tales.*

Mission Statement:

In general, we women wish to have complete control over both our husbands and our lovers and to be masters of all men.

* * * * *

Hodge was right. Claudia was there this Saturday morning, cheering her team. She looked pretty good, like she belonged on a movie set as the classic blond trophy wife of some robber baron. Then I remembered she is a movie star with 156 pornographic films to her credit. This year she received the Adult Times award for best actress in an adult film.

Me: "Are you Claudia Couvert?"

She: "If you are a goddamn process server, I swear to God I will punch you in the nose and give you a bloody nose, and then I will punch you in the mouth and give you bloody teeth!"

Me: "Hodge sent me. Hodge Hootman."

Claudia looked me over head to toe and toe to head, shook her head, and said, "Hodge needs to have his eyes examined. You don't have the body type for my movies, and you certainly don't have the equipment for my other business. Sorry, Baby Doll. It's a no-go."

"Claudia, I know that. I need to talk about something important. Hodge said you would be very interested."

She: "BEAT IT, KID! Can't you see I am busy supervising my team? I'm busy. Too busy. Leave me alone." She looked away to the field, cupped her mouth, and shouted, "OK, Mickey, let's see what you can do."

Mickey was at bat. He was no taller than the bat itself, and he seemed to be having difficulty lifting the bat effectively.

You could say the outlook wasn't brilliant for the RV Nine that day, a nice fresh, bright Saturday morning. The score was 37 to zero, with only one batter left in play. Mickey.

Mickey waved back at Claudia and turned to face the pitcher. The spheroid flew. To me, it looked high and outside, but the umpire cried, "Strike one!"

Mickey looked to us for consolamentum and shrugged his shoulders, doffed his hat, turned, and, with his overweight bat, hit home plate three times. With a determined face, he stared at the pitcher and nodded. To me, the next pitch looked too low and inside, but the umpire cried, "Strike two!"

Claudia screamed, "You're doing great, Mick. Hang in there, kiddo."

Mick swung and missed.

"You're out!" said the ump, and that was that.

Claudia gathered the kids. "Kiddoes, that was great playing. One of these days, we might come closer to winning. Winning is not the goal, not our goal. Baron Pierre de Coubertin, the founder of the modern Olympics in 1894, said that winning was not important. Participation is the goal. Participation is what counts and what is important. You, kiddoes, participated in the great American pastime. You played baseball! That is ten thousand times better than sitting at home on your asses watching some stupid kid show on TV where one clown is hitting another over the head with a pillow. You got in there and played baseball! I am proud of all of you. You came in second today. Let's hear it now—a big loud cheer for coming in second!"

There were only two teams, they and them. Now the losers, Claudia's bedraggled RV team, was cheering itself that they had come in second.

When the din dimmed down, Claudia said, "Kiddoes, it is easy to be a good winner. To be a good loser takes character. Show your good character by going over there and shaking the hands of each and every member of the winning team. They beat you fair and square and won this game because they played better than you did. Congratulate them and tell them you look forward to playing with them again. Show your good sportsmanship."

Claudia looked at me with an inquiring face. "You still here? Don't be a pain in the ass. I told you no film for you and no whoring. You just don't have it, Dollink. Unless, unless (she gave me the once over again), unless your chest took on a very new look. Even then, probably—no way!"

Me: "Yes, I know I'm unsuited to those professions. And, yes, I am still here. Please talk to me. Hodge said you would be very interested. How about this pain in the ass, namely me, treats you to lunch?"

Claudia's eyes brightened. She stroked her chin, looked up at the sky as if checking the weather, smacked her lips, and nodded. "Sounds good, Baby Doll. I'm famished. Lately, I've been too fucking busy and vice versa, too busy fucking, but I need to take a break for lunch. Watching the kids always gives me an appetite. I like the Mediterraneo Market and Café 1400 East NASA Road One. Meet me there in ten minutes. They have the best tiramisu in town."

* * * * *

We dined outdoors under a massive green umbrella. The waitress was a gigantic woman who spoke with what I thought was a Russian accent. Nope. She was Ukrainian, and the way she talked about the Russians indicated the Russians have lots to fear.

My lunch was a wonderful tuna salad sandwich consisting of tuna, olives, lettuce, tomato, cucumber, red onions, and French dressing. The best ever. Claudia had the baked kibbi plate cracked wheat mix with beef and pine nuts, and baba ghanoush. We both had the tiramisu, the best I ever tasted. It is billed as big enough for two people, but we each ate our own, working our way through three delicious layers. I will try to attach a picture. The strawberry on top of real whip cream was a nice touch.

Mediterraneo Market and Café Tiramisu

Of course, we talked about women's rights and the oppression. It was clear to me Claudia was all in and eager to help. She did have some advice, and I will let her speak for herself.

"Forget about using force. That is not a female thing. Violence in any form will not work. Guns? Forget it. Look at January 6th. They were highly motivated and better financed and organized than you think. Many were armed. Yet, they failed and failed miserably. So far, over 800 have pleaded guilty and are either in prison or awaiting sentencing. Thomas Webster just got ten years in prison and three subsequent years of supervision for assaulting a police officer with a flag pole. After three hours of deliberation, the jury found him guilty of all six counts. His claim of self-defense fell flat. His argument that he was the helpless victim of unscrupulous politicians promoting the idea the election was stolen fell flat. Any excuse they may give will be rejected. Violence is not your answer because it is not a female thing, and, furthermore, it will not work.

"With all their careful planning and aggressiveness and bravo, they, the Oath takers, MAGA maggots, election deniers, white supremacists, militia members, conspiracy theorists, Trump loyalists, and so forth, looted the capital, destroyed official documents, stole stuff, broke stuff, killed six, injured 136, tried to hang the Vice President of the United States, Mike Pence, and caused 2.6 million dollars worth of damage. The nation watched the fiasco on TV and watched the cops take over and win. Biden was confirmed as President despite their best efforts to reverse the election.

"If that group of nut cases and MAGA maggots could fail, there is no way an army of women could succeed. You would have to defeat the capital police, who are now on guard, the D.C. police, who are now on guard, the national guard, who will be called out, and you will have to defeat the United States Army, which is four plus in favor of democracy and the constitution. American generals didn't support Trump's attempted coup, and they won't support yours."

A pause. Complete silence while Claudia's words sunk in.

Me: "Oh, shit. You're right. Our whole scheme was stupid—mere blue smoke, a pipe dream that could never be, will never be. I feel terrible. I'm dizzy; my arms and legs are tingling and shaking, and my vision is dimmed. There's a pain in the center of my chest. I'm over breathing. You're right! God damn. You're right."

A nice woman, a grandmother type, at the table across the way supplied a paper bag for me to rebreathe into. She said, "I carry this around because I have hyperventilation attacks too. I learned the treatment from a movie where Jack Nicholson had an attack. It turns out he carries a bag because, in real life, he needs it." Our Ukrainian waitress appeared from nowhere with some Ozark bottled water. Claudia wiped my face with a cool, wet towel. That felt great. Woke me up.

When I had partly recovered, Claudia continued.

"What you told me about Meph-foe is interesting. I believe Meph-foe was right about taking advantage of biology, the difference, biologically speaking, between male and female. I have some ideas. Wanna hear them?"

Me: "OK. Can I have another drink of water? And keep the bag handy. I'm still trembling. I feel like vomiting. Jittering of the brain. An inner jittering. It's panic. I'm terrified the oppression will last forever. I'm a wreck. I am abject. I am a mess. An abject mess!"

She: "Abject Mess, how about being more sympathetic to the plight of men? They are part of our species. You need to treat them better. Don't be anti-men. Men are not just going to go away. You can't ignore them. Most of what they do is not exactly their fault. They are victims as much as you are. They are helpless in view of their evolutionary condition."

"Evolution? What has that to do with it?"

She: "Everything, doll. Evolution explains all the biology on this planet. If you don't believe in evolution, you're a fool. One of my Jesuit customers, Father Meyers, told me that. He said evolution is a fact. The only question is: did God have anything to do with it?

"Men evolved into what they are. In the long history of human development, men had to leave the cave and hunt and kill. They had to protect us females and the kids from wild animals and other aggressive tribes. Fighting and killing became their thing. The strong survived and reproduced, accounting for sexual dimorphism where females are smaller and eat less and males are bigger and eat more to stay stronger."

Me: "I'm not sure I follow you. Get to the point if you have one. More water, please. My stomach hurts right here. Might be gall bladder or appendix. May I have the bag again? No question, the bag treatment calms me down."

She: "Anxiety, kiddo. Just relax. You are over breathing, making your blood too alkalotic and lowering the circulating ionized calcium. Rebreathing your expelled air puts carbon dioxide back where it belongs—in you, makes the blood acid again, and normalizes the blood calcium. The pain will go—soon.

"My point, Horatio, is there are more things in heaven and earth than are dreamt of in your philosophy. Men are sick. They are sick because their genetic makeup is inappropriate to modern life. They have this natural instinct to fight and kill, but we don't need that kind of aggressiveness anymore.

"Because there are no longer natural ways for men to work off their aggressions, we get mass shootings, rapes, serial murders, useless wars, road rage, spouse abuse, you name it. Modern civilization has no need of such men. Remember professor Higgins in *My Fair Lady*? He complains, 'Why can't a woman be more like a man.' Flip that, and we get our complaint and the solution to male oppression: Why can't a man be more like a woman?"

Me: "So what? This is going nowhere. How can you make a man more like a woman?" I tried to stand but sat right down again. Too dizzy and nauseated.

She: "I don't know, but I think it will be easier than you think. Listen carefully, sweetie pie. I am about to solve your problem big time. Let's start with the well-known genetic disease, sickle cell anemia. I am going to use this disease as an analogy, as an example of what to do. Are you with me? Need some coffee?"

We signaled for cappuccinos, and Claudia continued. She seemed to know something, so I tried to follow while sipping my coffee. How in the world could we make a man more like a woman? I had the sinking feeling the mission was hopeless, and Claudia was off her rocker. The mission was a bust. Another attack was coming on, but I just held my breath. That should work just as well as the bag trick. Stop breathing. See what a fast learner I am?

She: "Normal people have a normal hemoglobulin which carries oxygen in the red cell to every cell in the body. People who have sickle cell disease have two doses of an abnormal hemoglobulin that causes the red blood cells to assume, under certain conditions, the shape of a sickle. People who have one dose of the sickle hemoglobulin are clinically normal and have the sickle trait. Most cases of sickle cell disease are in sub-Saharan Africa and in the U.S. people of African descent. How come? The answer is in the evolutionary adaptation to the environment. Sickle trait confers resistance to malaria. Get it? As humans evolved in a malaria environment, the sickle trait was selected for survival because it protected from the serious malaria. Now picture the situation here where there is no malaria. The sickle trait now becomes a liability. If two people with the sickle trait have a child, there is a 25% chance the child will have sickle cell disease and a 50% chance the child will have the sickle trait."

Me: "So what? I still don't get what you are driving at."

She: "The environment has changed, and the evolutionary condition that helped the survival of those with sickle trait no longer applies as malaria is no longer here in the United States. The same thing happened to men. They evolved in a different environment, one where killing and fighting was needed and greatly rewarded. Times are changed, and the aggressive masculine adaptation to modern life is inappropriate and wrong. Men, all men, are carrying, were born with, and are now afflicted by their genetic defect, a defect that now threatens to destroy civilization. That genetic defect is the Y chromosome. The Y makes men men and makes the hormones and the beards and the sperms and everything that is closely associated with manhood. The main problem is with men. There is nothing for them anymore. They can make money, but it isn't anywhere near the thrill of life-or-death battle.

"The cure for sickle cell anemia is to cut out the gene that causes the disease. The cure for masculine aggression, for their worship of guns and weapons and war and conflict, is to cure them of the genetic defect by getting rid of the Y chromosome."

Me: "Claudia, how come you know so much about this stuff?"

She: "Majored in biology at Vassar College, Poughkeepsie, New York."

Me: "Vassar? Isn't that one of the colleges no one gets into?"

She: "Yup. It's Seven Sisters, like Barnard, Pembroke, Smith, Radcliffe (absorbed in 1999 by Harvard), Mount Holyoke, Bryn Mawr, or Wellesley."

Me: "That's nine, not seven."

She: "Right. We always add Pembroke because it is connected with Brown. It's not Seven Sisters but should be. Radcliffe no longer exists, so that makes seven left. Most people don't know where the Seven Sisters idea comes from. It's the seven daughters of Titan Atlas, the Pleiades. See it? Vassar gave me a classical education. I feel like an intellectual giant among pigmies. The reason I feel that way is that I am an intellectual giant among pigmies. Most people know very little, and the little they know is often wrong. H. L. Menken, the bard of Baltimore, famously said, 'No one ever lost money betting on the ignorance of the American people.'"

"I don't know how I got into Vassar, but I did. The application had a page that said to type your autobiography here. I turned the page on the side and drew a beautiful picture of a cat sunning itself on the grass. The acceptance came by return mail. I guess the admissions officers were burned out reading puffed autobios, probably doctored 17 times by anxious parents. Vassar was the right school for me. Great education and wonderful campus with lots of grass and trees, plenty of good food in the cafeteria, nice dorms, friendly students, and great traditions. Around Christmas time, all us girls got out of the dorms and screamed our heads off. They called it the primal scream. Very therapeutic. You should try it when you get uptight. The other tradition I liked, I don't know if it still holds, was the requirement the girls wear white gloves and pearls to dinner. Very elegant. Legend has it, Jane Fonda, yes, she went to Vassar, came to dinner with her white gloves on but nothing else. Aside from gloves, she was nude. She was a renegade even back then. More power to her. We need more women like her. She did a great job in *Klute* as the high-priced call girl Bree Daniels, who is in a marvelous literary tradition of adventuresses like Scarlett O'Hara, Becky Sharp, Nana, and so forth who capture and enrapture readers. Jane learned the ropes from talking to madams and prostitutes. That's why she looked authentic. Got best actress for that in 1971. Blacklisting followed, and her trip to Hanoi in 1972 was a classic Jane Fonda affair. She gathered letters from the POWs and brought the letters home. She openly contradicted Nixon by affirming the POWs were not starving, were not tortured, and were not brainwashed. Adding, 'Anyone who says they are is a hypocrite and a liar.'"

Me: "WOW! Even then, she knew and tried to alert the public."

"The F.B.I. arrested her at the Cleveland International Airport on her return from an antiwar college speaking tour in Canada. I forget when that was. I think it was 1970 when she was known as Hanoi Jane. She was told the arrest was on direct orders from the White House. The little white pills they found and said were drugs turned out on chemical analysis to be vitamins. Case dismissed! My favorite picture is the 1977 *Fun with Dick and Jane*. It's a riot. Take a look at it. 'Harper, you can't buy a rubber plant with a rubber check.'"

Claudia opened her purse and pulled out her checkbook. "This one won't bounce. To whom shall I make the check? Grossly unfair gender disparities must be reversed. A woman must be free to determine her own destiny. Male aggression is the problem that needs to be contained. The future of civilization lies with women."

Claudia paused. Her face transmogrified and became hideous, and a strong war face emerged. She continued, her tone backed by wisdom and vast experience. "Women must heal wounds inflicted by a remorseless and cruel world. That's our mission. That's your mission. The future is in our hands." She held her hands out to me, the ancient gesture that was both an offering and an invitation to come forward, to embrace. I held her hands gently and smiled. I probably loved her too, in my fashion.

Got that? She said, "*To whom*." Who talks like that? Who says, "To whom shall I write the check?" No one but the Ivy League crowd and the Seven Sisters crowd. They answer when asked, "Who's there?"—"It's I, Claudia," whereas we normal people say, "It's me." Also, note the use of *shall* instead of *will*. "Shall" imposes an obligation and a duty. Will does not. Normal humans don't talk like this, only the intellectually elite, and Claudia is one among them, even though she is a porn star, a madam, and a whore.

"Please make it out to Houston Rollergirls, Inc. They are a tax-exempt charity, so your contribution is a tax deduction."

"Good. By the way, most of the organizations that funded the January 6th thing, according to representative Adam Kinzinger (Republican, Illinois), were tax-exempt charities. The government was indirectly supporting the rebellion. This country is SNAFU—situation normal all fucked up."

She handed me the check. My eyes popped out. It read Two Hundred Thousand Dollars. Gasp. "Claudia, many, many thanks. You are a gem."

"Thank the wives."

"The wives?"

"Yes, the wives keep me in business. Why do men come to me for something they can easily secure elsewhere for free. Why do married men go out for hamburger when they can get steak at home? One answer they give is that sex is their relaxation, and since they couldn't find it relaxing at home, they looked for it elsewhere. Some say their wives are good mothers and good cooks but indifferent bed partners. Others say that their mates are naggers and after a hard day at work, they needed companionship, not needling or bugging. 'I don't want to hurt my wife or family, but I have no outlet for my full emotions at home. If I took a mistress, there might be complications.' The feelings of my bachelor clientele could be summed up as: Why waste the effort wining-and-dining and sweet talking a girl just on the chance that you may score? Besides, an experienced girl, as I, Claudia, supply, is never a disappointment."

"It is my firm belief that 99 times out of 100, a wife could keep her husband on the ranch if she used half the effort to hold him that she did to hook him. When a woman sets her sights for a guy, she goes all out to be attractive. She keeps herself groomed to perfection. She always has that dab of perfume in the right place, just enough eye shadow, and so forth. She laughs at his jokes, goes along with his whims, and flirts with other men just enough to keep him on the bit. And whatever she does, she tries to convince him that it is all for the great wonderful Him.

"But after a girl gets a boy and has that ring on her finger, she forgets there are lots of girls at the office and that men will always be men. Why should a forty-dollar gold ring and a ten-dollar marriage license entitle her to turn off all that charm she had turned on during courtship? Why doesn't she continue to dress up for him? Why can't she use her eyes to see how he is feeling? Why can't she use her ears to listen to him? Why can't she use her tongue to compliment him and involve him in interesting conversation? And here's a main point: Why, after waving her sex like a red cape to him, doesn't she at least pretend to enjoy his caresses? Instead of criticizing them, I should thank such wives for keeping me in business.

"Why wouldn't such a man turn from his wife to my girls, who are always beautifully groomed and lovely to look at and gay and responsive, who are always flattering him, telling him what a terrific lover he is? Of course, they are getting paid for it. But doesn't a wife get paid also? From my vantage, I see a prostitute is anyone who sells themselves for gain. Women who take a husband not out of love but out of greed, to get their bills paid, to get a fine house and clothes and jewels, to get out of a boring job, or away from disagreeable and nosey parents, to avoid being an old maid—these are whores in everything but a name. The difference is my girls give a man his money's worth. They have to in view of all the competition from amateurs these days.

"Yes, I admit, there is one man in a hundred who couldn't be kept on the ranch by a harem of beautiful wives. And unfortunately, there are some wives who do their best but just don't have enough of the old Eve. In my opinion, most women lose their husbands to other women because the other woman licked them in the hay."

* * * * *

Whew. Claudia is something. I wish I knew as much, and if I get the chance, I will devote my life to getting cultured and learned. The key to success in America, as I see it, is education. I mean real success. Not the success from making money in every way but working for it. Claudia's ideas were right on. I sent Malice a message that the money was coming and that she and the Rollergirls should hold off on buying weapons and await further orders. The mission was the same, but the plans had changed. If this were a novel, we would be at plot point two, where things veer off in a different direction or there is a change in outlook. But this is not a novel. It's a history. Nevertheless, we are changing direction and outlook. The mission is the same, but the method will be different. We were now on our way to a solid female victory, a victory without bloodshed and a victory complete beyond our wildest dreams and imaginations.

CHAPTER THE LAST

"Man is but a reed, the weakest thing in nature, but he is a thinking reed."

—Blaise Pascal

To eliminate the Y chromosome was logically possible and physically possible, but at the time, not technically possible. Therefore, we needed to do some serious thinking; we needed expert help. The experts were two post-docs in the famous laboratory of molecular genetics at the Texas Children's Hospital. Post-docs are notoriously underpaid and overworked, so they were happy to help solve our Y-chromosome problem working on weekends and nights, provided we paid them well, and of course, we did pay them well with Claudia's money laundered through the roller derby ladies.

Doctor Hootman set up the lab adjacent to his clandestine clinic. Our post-docs were quite at home there and thought the lab was every bit as good as the lab of their day job, and they thought the noise level was less, and they thought they could really accomplish more because there were no administrative hassles and they didn't have to go to boring faculty meetings where professors just mouthed off ad nauseum because the profs liked to hear themselves talk.

No need to go into the scientific method used. This has been published in *Nature* and in *The Journal of the American Association for the Advancement of Science*. Consult the journal articles for details. Here I will summarize the ideas so you know what happened.

It turns out the y chromosome is on the way out. Its complete extinction is in the cards because it cannot renew itself as the other chromosomes can. All therian mammals are losing their y chromosome, not just human men. In fact, voles and Japanese spiny rats no longer have a Y. Perhaps the traits that helped y survive are no longer as helpful as they were in helping fit males for survival. Who knows? Perhaps some new traits like working and playing well with others better fit more men to get a good mate. When the environment changed from primitive dog-eat-dog to make nice, the genes that supported violence tended to drop out in favor of genes that make nice. Actually, that is one of the current ideas about why genes on the Y chromosome are being lost. Or, perhaps some environmental factor as yet unidentified has caused the y to shrink. Fossil evidence shows the proto-y was once as big as the X chromosome. As time went by, it shrank, and instead of looking like an X, or even a Y, it now, under the microscope, looks like an amorphous blob. Not only is the y involuting, but human sperm counts are on the decline as well. This may pose a serious problem for human reproduction in the future, but it is hard to say when. Some scientists say in 4.6 million years; other scientists say in ten years. Here's the fact to think about: Of the original 1,438 genes on the y chromosome, only 1,393 remain. Why these genes have disappeared and what they previously encoded for in the way of proteins is not known. The loss is real, but the reason or reasons for the loss is not clear. From the larger evolutionary perspective, we would conclude some male traits are being deselected. Consequently, some males don't get to mate and therefore do not pass along their genes.

Normal humans do not need a Y chromosome to live. Witness women who are alive and well and have no Y. Also, as men age, some of them lose the Y chromosome. A recent study from Norway showed the loss increases after age 75. In that study, LOY (loss of Y) was defined as finding 18% of the man's stem cells without a Y. LOY correlated with age, loss of vitality, and with decreased viable sperms and also predicts a lifespan on the average 5.5 years below expected. But the scientists think the lost life is due to some systemic factors and not due to the loss of the Y itself. In other words, loss of Y has no effect on life span. Correlation doesn't mean cause and effect. LOY die sooner, but not because their Y chromosomes are missing.

With the help of a professor at Baylor College of Medicine, a virus was made that was very infectious but caused no signs or symptoms. Our moonlighting post-docs engineered this virus to conjugate to the surface receptors on the Y chromosome and leave all other chromosomes intact. The conjugation causes the Y to involute, and the debris is cleared by the usual cellular processes.

Thus, our post-docs working in our secret laboratory turned mere chemicals and a common virus into gold, as though at the touch of a philosopher's stone.

Bingo! We were in. We had a coronavirus type A (there are four types: A, B, C, and D) that spread quickly from human to human and selectively destroyed the Y chromosome. Each person harboring this virus became a biological incubator that multiplied the viral agent and spread it throughout the body and then spread it to other people. We were about to change the world without actually having to kill anyone. Whoopee!

Initially, I was worried because the technique left men with only one functional X chromosome per cell, and I thought women had two. Two X seemed to me the natural setup, and I was concerned that men having only one X might have problems.

Post-doc Usha (with a slight smile) explained: "Jesus, Lollipop, what you don't know about human biology could fill volumes. All normal females have two X chromosomes as embryos. Before birth, one of the X chromosomes is inactivated. The inactivation is entirely random, so the female is left with only one active X in each somatic cell. According to the Lion Hypothesis, now a fact, on average, half of her active X chromosomes come from her father and half from the mother. The inert inactive chromosome appears under the microscope as a clump of chromatin called the Barr body, named after Murray Barr. Rest assured, men who have only one functioning X will look phenotypically normal. They have to because science is always right."

Me: "Phenotypically normal? Meaning what?"

Usha: "Phenotype refers to the sum of a living organism's observable traits and characteristics. After the Agent Freedom gets finished with them, men will look the same as they did before and will resemble and be normal humans because men and women are pretty much the same. They are, after all, the same species: homo sapiens. Fear not. Science is always right. Men and women will both have one active X chromosome per somatic cell. That will be the normal state for them and for everyone from now until doomsday."

Note from editor: The movement named the virus conjugate *Agent Freedom* because they thought the agent would liberate women from oppression and would, at the same time, free men from the genetic disease caused by the presence of the Y chromosome.

* * * * *

O.K. As they say, the rest is history. The liberating agent was distributed in every way we could think of: via propaganda that masks were useless, via roller ladies infecting themselves and spreading the virus, and by dumping the agent in reservoirs, water treatment plants, and dropping it on whole cities from the air. Within a month, most of the people in the United States had the virus, but they didn't know it because, remember? It caused no signs or symptoms. It behaved like the trillions of viruses already present in normal humans—viruses that do nothing or help preserve some vital functions as symbionts. As Professor Samo predicted, our virus spread just as fast as Covid-19 because it, too, was a coronavirus.

Slowly but surely, a mitigation effect occurred in the usual behaviors of men. Men were kinder and nicer. They became gentlemen in the original sense of the word. They began to work and play well with others. Mass shootings stopped. The daily carnage caused by gun violence, what Meph-foe had talked about, disappeared. Around the world, all wars stopped. Soldiers woke up one morning and decided they would make a separate peace. Most of them couldn't figure out, even in retrospect, why they had started fighting or what the war was all about. Now it seemed a colossal waste of time, money, energy, and life. Minatory men everywhere were deposed as completely and curiously out of step with modern life and feeling. Men everywhere were stepping to the sounds of a different drummer. Professional football—gone forever. Men were no longer interested in watching this brutal sport, nor would they watch boxing. Men were no longer interested in playing football, even for their previously absurd pay of multimillions. Football and boxing, and every brutal so-called sport died natural deaths. Good riddance. I rather doubt that football ever made any contribution to the improvement of the human race or human culture.

Instead of men wasting their lives watching some fool carry a pigskin down a field against determined opposition (sounds downright silly, doesn't it), they now spend the time chatting with their wives, or playing with the kids, or taking the family to the beach or on a picnic. Men even started knitting clubs and helped their wives with cooking, cleaning, shopping, washing, and baby and pet care. Gardening clubs sprung up all over, where men and women enjoyed talking with each other about the secret lives of the vegetables. Social dances became the rage again, especially rhumba and foxtrot.

Originally, I had the idea we would have to confiscate weapons. Wrong! Most men were no longer interested in guns. They threw their guns in the lakes and rivers to get them out of the home because they now considered any kind of gun too dangerous to have around.

However, there were pockets of resistance. There had to be resistance, particularly in the Midwest red states. There can be no light without shadow or no shadow unless there is light. This is something you can depend on: There will always be alliances of one kind or another, usually alliances of the stupid.

Letters and telegrams were received from these former MAGA maggots that stated absurd things like, "To get my gun, you will have to pry my dead fingers off the weapon." Isn't it amazing how some people stick their foot in the shit! What phony courage. Shameful too. Well, they asked for it, and we gave it to them.

The Roller Troops had to put down the rebellion just the way George Washington had to send in the troops to put down the Whisky Rebellion of 1794. But instead of the 13,000 militiamen Washington led to battle against 500 Pennsylvania farmers, we used 25 magnificent Roller Troops.

Our ladies are as agile as squirrels and as moving targets, impossible to hit with conventional rifles. We suffered no combat injuries except Kami Kazzi lost one of her four roller wheels on the right foot, fell, hit her forehead smack in the center, and has a hematoma there, looking like a modified eye of Shiva.

With the men, a different story. Their bodies are so easily damaged, so easily disposed of, water and a few chemicals (that's all they are), hardly more than a fly stuck and dying on some fly paper. I wonder how such humans appear to an electron, just a pile of bone, flesh, twisted proteins, nothing much.

Malice in Wonderland rejected the idea of arming her girls with AK-47s and the like in favor of the Street Sweepers, pictured below if I can find the space.

The infamous Street Sweeper Shotgun. Also known as the Armstel Striker. Malice read about it in her favorite magazine, *Soldier of Fortune.*

Developed by Hilton Walker in what was Rhodesia in 1980, the striker has a 12 gauge, 12-round revolving cylinder that fires all the rounds in 3 seconds! The cylinder rotates by the stored energy of a tension spring that must be wound by a special key. The gun was adopted and used by South African police and Israeli police and made its way to the United States via an advertising campaign by Cobray.

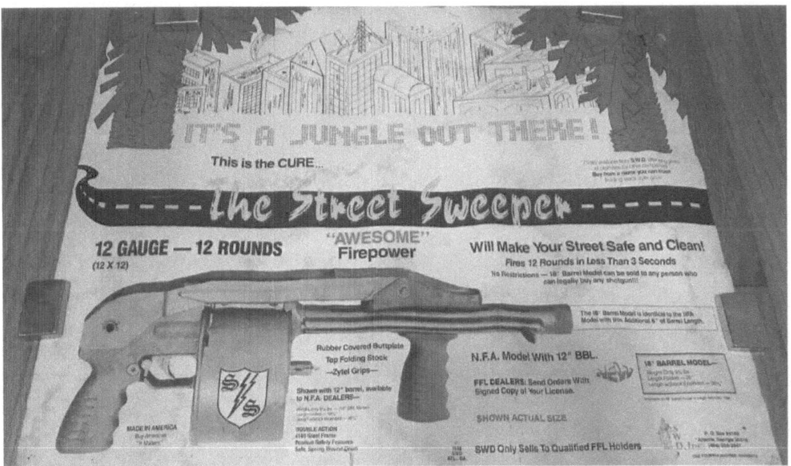

Notice the ad says, "The Street Sweeper will make your street safe and clean." It certainly did that for our Roller Troops, who dubbed it their "Ladies Home Companion."

In the old days before the *unpleasantness*, ATF didn't like the sweeper, calling it "a destructive device" due to "the lack of any sporting purpose." In other words, you can't take it on a duck hunt. But, of course, in America, there is always a loophole. Ex post facto law is not allowed. Therefore, sweepers already owned are legal now and forever. We just bought them all up with Claudia's money and paid a $200 federal transfer tax to get delivery. The gun required very little training and no practice on the range. You just pointed it in the direction you wished and fired away and mowed them down, clearing the street. According to Malice, "It was a perfect short-range military area arm, perfect for us. It worked exactly as stated in *Soldier of Fortune*."

But that was not enough, so we invented the demonstration. The idea was to show a superweapon that would convince any reasonable man to give up and surrender. The same idea was used on the Japanese during World War II. Two atomic bombs convinced the Japanese to surrender even though America had no more A-bombs to throw at them. The Japs didn't know that fact. It was top secret.

The demonstration aired on TV. Twelve male and twelve female rats under a bell jar were suddenly exposed to the *superweapon* we said would only kill the males. A puff went in, and all the male rats (identified with a black spot on their backs) dropped dead. Female rats just continued doing their rat thing. Seeing is believing, as they say. People pretty much believe anything they see or hear on TV. They believed what they thought they saw—namely that we had a superweapon and we could, at will, kill all males.

But what they really saw was quite different. They saw Doctor Hootman's experiment repeated over and over with mice, pigs, monkeys, and so forth. The males all died, and the females all lived because (did you guess this?) all the females got the antidote before they got the VX, and all the males got nothing.

Consolidation of power was what we were after with this ruse, and we got it. All governments and all businesses use some deceptions. This was ours. The women historians of the future will debate and decide if the demonstration was really needed or justified or both. In my opinion, it helped secure our objective: That government of women, by women, and for women shall not perish from the earth.

Men were not the only males cured of their affliction. Boys started jumping rope with the girls and playing hopscotch. Boys welcomed girls in traditional male games like handball, stickball, stoopball, baseball, and so forth. Some boys abandoned their little toy trucks and played with dolls. Others completely junked any kind of video war game and threw out their toy soldiers. They just were not interested in that stuff anymore. In school, they took electives in sewing, cooking, and touch typing. A whole new world of fun and pleasure was opened to them.

The most outstanding change occurred in those backwater and dark regions of Earth where women had been terribly suppressed. These accomplishments will be covered soon. Meanwhile, I am just busting with wanting to tell what happened in Washington, D.C.

A general election put me in charge for four years with the option of running for office again once more. I changed my name from Lollipop to Queen Azura after those Flash Gordon pictures with Buster Crabb. People started calling me Your Highness, which I hated, but what can you do? We abolished all nation states creating a one-world government named Lady Land. Our brave new world was better, much better, but not perfect. Some women were catty and jealous, and well, you get the picture. Nothing in this wide world of humans is 100% anything.

Queen Azura holds court upon which I wanted to model my court.

Only kidding.

Major policy issues arose about what to do with the former government's symbols. I favored complete destruction of the memorials to men and removal of the Washington Monument. The White House had to go, in my view, because it was an institution that let the number one world's most powerful male live in palatial luxury while most of the women of the world lived in abject poverty. The council overruled me, and the White House became a national museum designed to illustrate the excessive lifestyle of the patriarchs now deposed. If in D.C., come visit. Admission is free.

The day of the demolition of the phallic Washington Monument was made a national holiday. In its place, there arose a gigantic golden statue of Athena Parthenos, the goddess of wisdom, the arts, and classical learning. She symbolized our deep commitment to wisdom, knowledge, and science.

Our current focus is on climate change because our coastal cities are subsiding due to groundwater extraction while, at the same time, they are threatened by rising sea levels. There have been way too many wildfires, too many droughts, too many floods, too many hurricanes, and too many serious heat waves.

We women do share the difficulties with long-term thinking. We are not perfect. We are humans. Even when our shorelines are disappearing, when flooding and radically high temperatures are palpable in our cities, when droughts make water scarce and increase tensions, when mass migrations that began from war-torn regions cause conflicts, with ever scarcer resources, we still put off the decision-making that would change course on human-induced climate change.

It is hard to believe that former President Trump said climate change is a "hoax" and he withdrew the nation from the Paris accord. The reign of the phallus was indeed the reign of anti-science, idiocy, misinformation, and bullshit. The damage this jackass did is beyond the beyonds.

I hope it is not too late to reverse the anthropogenic warming of our planet. We must succeed, or humanity is doomed.

Report Card:

OK. As promised, I will review some of the many benefits that occurred worldwide as a result of the change of the guard and the takeover by women.

This is just a small list of the profound ramifications of the reign of women. It is hard to imagine the oppression that women endured in the old days. Women were whipped for showing some of their beauty in public. Mothers were lined up before firing squads because they taught their daughters how to read and write. In the Maldives, women were said not to have a soul. Therefore, they were not allowed to pray or go to the Friday Mosque. As they had no soul, they were property just like animals and bought and sold. The same thing in Papua, where ten dog teeth would buy a woman or a cow. Fifteen dog teeth bought a woman if the woman had a good work record.

India: ritual widow suicide abolished. If the husband died, the wife was expected to throw herself on the funeral pyre. No more. Sale of girls by brokers. No more. Dowry deaths where a woman was murdered right after marriage so the husband could keep her dowry. No more. Rapes—25,000 reported rapes every three days in north India. In Delhi, there were reported over 300 rapes a day and 700 harassments. No more. Child marriage, often against the girl's wish. No more. Nitric acid thrown in the face, causing blindness and permanent disfigurement. No more. Acid attacks were also common in Pakistan. No more. Women treated like children or property. No more.

Cameroon: Breast ironing where over 50% of girls had breasts burned on the idea that if they didn't have breasts, they couldn't tempt men. No more.

Guatemala: Over 700 women murdered each year. Most of the murderers never brought to justice. No more. The second highest rate of female HIV after sub-Saharan Africa. No more.

Saudi: Women unable to drive without a male relative on board. No more. Women not able to vote for high officials. No more.

Sudan, Somalia, Djibouti, Ethiopia, Kenya, Egypt, Mali, Central African Republic, Nigeria, Zaire, Cameroon, Chad, and Libya. Niger, Nigeria, Dahomey, Togo, Ghana, Upper Volta, Ivory Coast, Liberia, Sierra Leone, Guinea, Gambia, Senegal, Mauritania, Indonesia, Persian Gulf, United Arab Republic, Oman, Bahrein, South Yemen, Pakistan, and Russia (only a few ethnic groups): Clitorectomy and infibulation. No more. Hard to imagine so many countries had female genital mutilation, but they did. Why? Who knows? Probably they were trying to control female libido and thereby control females and suppress them.

Worldwide: no more wage inequality. No more job discrimination. No more restrictions on women by universities and institutions of learning. No more laws controlling what women do with their bodies or what they wear in public, who they love, what they read, or say or write.

Vale:

Here ends my history of how women saved civilization. Some things were left out, and some were toned down. I am sorry the story did not end with an exciting car chase. But what could I do? Peace and prosperity reigned and reigns in Lady Land. There is less drama but more fun and happiness.

In a sense, we accomplished what some medieval clerics and philosophers longed for: A world where there was but one sex. That was why Origen castrated himself at age 20 to "give up that which determined he was a man." Abelard said his castration was "more a blessing than a curse." It symbolized not merely his punishment for his imperfections, enabling him now beyond desire and beyond suspicion to pursue his pious purpose. His letters to Heloise resounded with belated monastic conviction, and he became a champion of celibacy.

See, some men loved being cured of their manhood even way back then. We did them a service, and in the process, we saved civilization.

Goodbye and good luck.

Your friend,

Lollipop

NOTE FROM THE PUBLISHER

Lollipop is the pen name of an American nuclear scientist who made major contributions to the development and deployment of thermonuclear weapons now known as Hydrogen or H bombs. His fundamental idea was to unite fission and fusion such that the fission reaction sparked the fusion. By placing fission/fusion in tandem, it became possible to make a thermonuclear weapon of any size, even large enough to destroy this planet. The National Academy of Sciences also credits him with the invention of using Lithium-6 deuteride as the fusion fuel. It is easier to handle than deuterium or tritium and, under the extreme temperatures of the weapon, breaks down to the unstable isotopes of hydrogen, which fuel the reaction.

After viewing the complete destruction of Eugelab in Eniwetok atoll November 1, 1952, by America's first hydrogen bomb, Lollipop began to consider his philosophical position as "untenable" and, after the Tsar Bomb in 1961 (flash seen 630 miles away, ten times more powerful than all the munitions used in World War II, blast wave circled Earth three times! And so forth), he resigned to dedicate his time and life to creative writing to "try to make a cowardly amends for the evil I have done."

STATEMENT BY THE AUTHOR

This work originally started as a disquisition on the abuse of women through the ages. It soon morphed into something much larger and more important when I realized most, if not all, of the violence in this wide world is due to one thing and one thing only: Male dominance and control.

Women, in general, are kind and gentle, and nurturing and would not even think of making or deploying weapons of mass destruction like thermonuclear bombs or nerve gases.

Small pockets of resistance, especially in the red states, called for the argument of force and were taken care of by the Roller Derby troops. Furthermore, we, much to our discredit, had to use VX nerve gas as a false and fake demonstration of our supreme power. The women historians of the future will decide if that demo was justified or not. Queen Azura, aka Lollipop, in my view, made sure our brave new world wouldn't spiral out of control. You agree?

How many serial killers are women? How many mass murderers are women? How many of the wars of our time and all time were organized, initiated, and sponsored by women? The fault, dear Brutus, is not in the stars but in ourselves that we let men, with their disposition to violence, control things.

After much study and contemplation, I arrived at the conclusion that most of the horrors of the world are the work products of the minds of minatory men who (like Pol Pot, Mao, Hitler, Stalin, Putin, Kim, Xi, Castro, Henry VIII, Caesar, Octavian, and Nero) have caused much misery and pain and suffering. What do you think of my conclusion?

Incontrovertible, right?

Think of this: Many people think the cause of gun violence is the availability of guns. In a sense, that may be true, but in a larger sense, it isn't. Guns just sit there doing nothing until someone, usually a man, picks up the gun and fires it with the definite intent of killing people. Therefore, the real cause of gun violence is not guns per se but the men who use them. And the men, poor miserable things, are themselves a victim of nature. They were born with a significant chromosomal defect, the Y chromosome, which has now become evolutionarily anachronistic and in need of radical excision treatment.

But remember this: Men's genetic defect was no more their fault than sickle cell anemia is the fault of someone native to west Africa, and no more men's fault than hemophilia is the fault of those who suffer from it. Men were born that way with that terrible genetic defect without their knowledge or consent. They deserve to be pitied, not despised.

After working on the disquisition on the abuse of women starting from Eve and going up to 2022 (there is lots to say on the subject), it came to me that modern society was headed to self-destruction and now had the physical means to destroy itself and our planet in the World War III that was being orchestrated and choreographed by Russia in Ukraine.

China, Russia, North Korea, and Saudi Arabia were controlled by minatory men ruling by decree, dictators obsessed with power, and military aggression. In the past decade, for instance, Beijing built a 21st-century military, absorbed Hong Kong in violation of treaties, threatened to attack Taiwan, constructed a constellation of militarized islands in the South China Sea, gained strategic footholds in Latin America, Southeast Europe, Africa, and Asia. Beijing has mushroomed its stockpile of nuclear weapons, brandished an arsenal of space-based weapons, and exploited cyberspace to wage a hack-and-harvest assault against U.S. industry. My social dance friend, Ai Ping (her name means "loves peace"), says the communists have unleashed a high-tech Orwellian surveillance state at home, thuggishly levering the pandemic for geopolitical advantage. This is a nightmare society where the state monitors, controls, and punishes everything it dislikes. There, Big Brother is always watching and always listening. Ai Ping says video cameras even pick up and send tickets to the jaywalkers identified by their faces as they cross the street. Dissenters disappear overnight, and their families can't find out where they are or what happened to them. She witnessed an official kidnapping right there in Tiananmen Square.

Russia—same sad story. Russia devolved from a fledgling democracy and partner in stabilizing Europe in the 1990s into an authoritarian regime bent on the reconstitution of the old Russian Empire. Post-Soviet Russia's path—invasion of Georgia and Ukraine, military deployments and combat ops in the Middle East, nuclear threats against NATO members, weaponized natural gas—all that speaks for itself. In today's Russia, the kleptocrats, the military, and internal security forces run a regime that rules by decree and completely controls all public information sources.

Like a modern-day Cassandra, I saw and offered a glimpse of what the future looks like, and what lies ahead. Everything looked bleak, and I was an optimist. And then I had an idea.

This terrible fate could be avoided by deposing men from power and placing women in command. How to do this became the subtext of my work, and I realized the largest possible audience for this idea would result if the discussion used novelistic techniques to outline in exact detail a fictional account of how women supposedly took over the world and saved civilization. I wanted to create a relatively short novel, less tendentious, more American, and above all interesting and conversational using demotic, the language of the people, to produce an exciting drama wherein the women sympathetically and completely take over the world and save civilization.

Never in a billion billion years did I imagine that the strategic and tactical methods detailed in the novel would activate the women's avulsion (which the movement subsequently renamed and reframed *The Unpleasantness*) that saved us all for all time. Complete and total elimination of male rule had to be the sine qua non of what we had to do to ensure permanent peace. The few men like myself and Hodge and Doctor Hootman and Professor Samo who were permitted to survive will soon go the way of all flesh, and that will leave a world entirely populated by women. That is the aim, and that is the desired effect: Women's World, a world entirely populated by women and only women.

May I crow about my achievement? My work is like that of Henry David Thoreau, only bigger and better. Thoreau lived on a kettle hole left from ancient glaciers and wrote up the experience in his book *Walden; or, Life in the Woods.*

That book and his famous essay on civil disobedience, illegal but non-violent activity and protest, as expressed by Thoreau, energized the American Civil Rights Movement, the liberation of India from the British, the establishment of the Irish Free State, and freedom for South African blacks.

Thoreau refused to pay taxes on the basis that the money supported slavery through federal and Supreme Court permission, and the taxes also supported the Mexican War of 1848, which he hated.

Thoreau was imprisoned for failure to pay those taxes, and, famously, he was visited by Ralph Waldo Emerson, the high priest of transcendentalism, who asked, "Henry, why are you here in prison?" To which Thoreau replied, "the real question, Waldo, is why are you on the outside?"

Now that society and government are under complete female control, we can all rest assured that peace and happiness must follow. Notice how all gun violence stopped overnight, and the war in Europe disappeared because no one was interested in guns, killing, or even fighting. Unexpected was the sudden and rapid decline in fatal traffic accidents. In Texas alone, 2,345 deaths per year went to six. That fact points to male egos somehow being involved in fatal crashes.

Female leadership offered, in my view, the soundest guide to the health of soil and soul, the most reliable respite from disaster, dispute, and despair. Women are not perfect, and their rule has had problems. But the world is a thousand times better off than it had been. I hope you agree.

Ladies, you may miss brutish men, but not that much. And in a short while, shorter than you think, you won't miss them at all.

POSTSCRIPT BY LOLLIPOP

After the publication of this history, I received an interesting letter from a housewife in what used to be Kansas. She wanted to know how voles and the Japanese spiny rats survive as a species when they have no Y chromosome.

Usha set to work on the problem and discovered SRY, the gene that regulates, controls, and makes for male reproductive function, had migrated, in these two species, to another chromosome where it was functional and protected. If Usha has the time and energy, she will explain in a short disquisition the mechanics of gene editing for the interest of some of you readers who want to know more details. With the new techniques, humans will soon have complete control of their genetic material. And that is good news for the people who suffer from the 180,000+ known genetic diseases.

The fact is by a wonderful feat of biological engineering (clustered regularly interspaced palindromic repeats—CRISPR), the same that was evolutionarily done for voles and rats was done for our men. So now we have our cake, and we can eat it too. The new class of men has all the reproductive power of the old class minus all the genes that let to abuse, bullying, killing, violence, and so forth. The undesirable traits promoted by the Y genes are gone, gone forever. Human SRY now safely resides on chromosome 12.

Thus, happy days are here again. We have love, sex, kindness, and gentleness from a new type of man who lacks all of the old genes that led to violence. We got our men back, but they, emotionally, are more like us women and into love and romance and affection and kindness and peace and good food and dance and good drinks and fun—just like us.

HOORAY!

FINAL WORDS BY DOCTOR GEORGE HOOTMAN

Friends and physicians, I am not like the pirate Captain Hook in Peter Pan, who was always giving his last final speech because he thought he might be about to die.

I am not about to die, but I do want to get in my last final words. Like Cherry Bomb, my favorite song is *Regrette Rien* by Edith Piaf because that's the way I feel. I regret nothing and would do it all over again the same way. To clarify my ethical position, let me quote the code of medical ethics of the American Medical Association (reference; *New England Journal of Medicine*, 387:11 page 959):

"In some cases, the law mandates conduct that is ethically unacceptable. When physicians believe a law violates ethical values or is unjust, they should work to change the law. In exceptional circumstances of unjust laws, ethical responsibilities should supersede legal duties."

The question I faced was what to do when the law requires me to harm a patient. When the law in Texas directly and immediately threatened the health of my patient, I had no qualms about disobeying the law and doing what was right. After all, it is I who had to face myself each day while shaving. How could I look in the mirror? How could I face myself if I had not done what I thought was right and good and just?

The Mississippi law at issue in the recent Supreme Court case Dobbs v. Jackson Women's Health Organization called elective abortions carried out after 15 weeks of gestation "demeaning to the medical profession." The majority of the justices (5 out of 9, 55.6%) agreed, claiming that the state's law banning such abortions would preserve "the integrity of the medical profession." Just the opposite is true. Major medical groups have argued that it's the court's decision in

Dobbs that demeans and threatens the integrity of the profession since laws banning abortion can compel doctors to choose between harming patients and breaking the law.

Before the justices reached their erroneous decision about how the profession feels about the case and the issue, they might have consulted those in the know, the doctors themselves. Here's what organized medicine has to say (reference: New England Journal of Medicine, ibid. page 960):

The American Medical Association called Dobbs "an egregious allowance of government intrusion into the medical examination room, a direct attack on the practice of medicine and the patient-physician relationship, and a brazen violation of patients' rights to evidence-based reproductive health services."

The American Academy of Family Physicians wrote that the decision "negatively impacts our practices and our patients by undermining the patient-physician relationship and potentially criminalizing evidence-based medical care."

The American College of Physicians stated, "A patient's decision about whether to continue a pregnancy should be a private decision made in conjunction with a physician or other health care professional, without interference from the government."

The CEO of the American College of Obstetricians and Gynecologists called Dobbs "tragic" for patients, "the boldest act of legislative interference that we have seen in this country." and "an affront to all that drew my colleagues and me into medicine."

Medical organizations are rarely so united. Even many physicians who oppose abortion recognize that medically nuanced decisions are best left in the hands of individual patients and their physicians.

Civil disobedience is a nonviolent, conscientious act contrary to law, carried out with the aim of bringing about a change in an unjust law. The best-known proponents of civil disobedience are

Henry David Thoreau (mentioned by our nuclear scientist in his note to the readers), Mahatma Gandhi, and Martin Luther King, Jr.

King argued people must respect the law. But he also wrote, "law and order exist for the purpose of establishing justice," and he agreed with Saint Augustine that "an unjust law is no law at all." King described a "moral responsibility to disobey unjust laws."

I applaud the medical profession's wide civil disobedience when Dutch physicians collectively turned in their licenses rather than practice under Nazi rule. I applaud the physicians who resigned from the CIA when the organization became involved in "enhanced interrogation" (namely torture). Similar disobedience may be required to repair the moral fabric of our country and the integrity of our profession, should we suffer damage like that injudiciously inflicted upon us by a Supreme Court or any other power or authority figure. Eternal vigilance is the price of liberty, and we must be eternally vigilant.

ONE LAST THING ABOUT WHAT PUTS IVF IN THE POST–ROE BATTLEFIELDS

The creation and destruction of embryos is the issue that spooks the antiabortion people. To maximize the chance of fertilization and a successful pregnancy, I had to fertilize as many of a woman's eggs as were retrieved. After a few days, some of those fertilized eggs may stop growing, in which case they are discarded. Embryologists then assess the growing embryos for quality, zeroing in on those that are viable and could potentially create a healthy pregnancy. Embryos that are not viable are destroyed as well. If an individual or a couple opts for genetic screening, they may choose to get rid of embryos that would result in a diseased child.

Finally, couples face the choice of what to do with leftover embryos once they have completed their family. They may discard them, continue paying storage fees ($695/year), or, less commonly, donate them to scientific research or to a couple seeking "embryo adoption," a practice religious groups encourage. Couples who don't want more children who are uncomfortable with or morally opposed to discarding or storing embryos and don't want their biological children born to someone else opt for a "compassionate transfer": inserting the embryo into a person's uterus at a time when she isn't fertile, and the embryo is unlikely to attach.

Here's the problem: Under a legal framework that gives a fertilized egg personhood rights no matter its location, any destruction of an embryo deemed viable by the state would be termed a serious crime, potentially including murder. Even a doctor overseeing an embryo that didn't thaw successfully could face lawsuits or criminal charges. Liquid nitrogen storage tanks do fail for several reasons: The temperature alarms may fail, as in the Cleveland Clinic, and the embryos will die. The automatic liquid nitrogen filler may fail, and the embryos will die. The tank may leak, and the embryos will die, and so forth. Hundreds of lawsuits have been filed by couples who lost their embryos and their chance to have a family. Very sad, no question. That is the problem with medicine in general: Some things can go wrong and often do. In my view, even getting out of bed in the morning can cause problems. We get up and leave the bedroom because the benefits outweigh the risks. We do IVF because the benefits outweigh the risks for couples who need or want children. I hope you agree.

DISQUISITION ON CRISPR BY USHA

What you are about to read is the absolutely simplest way this new biology can be explained. The complexity is not my fault, but the fault of nature as that is what is there, the reality of gene functioning and editing—very complicated and very powerful and very useful.

Bacteria have been trained to make medically useful proteins like human insulin, human growth hormone, human somatostatin, human alpha -1 antitrypsin, human albumin, and monoclonal antibodies. These engineered human proteins are exceptionally pure and are used worldwide as therapies.

Plants such as rice and wheat have been engineered to grow faster, produce more nutritious food, and be disease and insect-resistant. New cows and new salmons and new pigs and new goats have been made that help sustain the food supply. There is even a pet fish, a GMO fish—the GloFish, now available in pink, orange-yellow, green, purple, and red. The green fluorescent gene from a jellyfish is inserted into the fish embryo to make a green, a red gene from a sea coral makes red fluorescence. These are popular pets. In the spring of 2003, Taiwan authorized the sale of GMO fish as pets. Within a month, over 100,000 fish had been sold for USD $18.60 each.

CRISPR

Microorganisms use CRISPR and CRISPR-associated proteins (Cas) to fight viruses through recognition and destruction of specific DNA sequences. We use the same as a transformative technology to treat, cure, and prevent human disease.

HOW DOES CRISPR WORK?

This technology allows scientists to change DNA sequences in cells at virtually any desired position, enabling fundamental research and therapeutic applications. CRISPR-Cas9, the most widely used genome editor, is an RNA-guided DNA-cutting enzyme that makes double-stranded DNA breaks at preselected target positions. Repair of the break site results in either small insertions and deletions (Indels) introduced by error-prone repair or the insertion of a DNA donor sequence chosen by the doctor (homology-directed repair). Indels are useful for interrupting gene function, whereas sequence insertion can replace a defective sequence to restore normal gene function.

We now have a tool kit of several proteins related to Cas9 that can do amazing things for us. These include genome editors that can change single nucleotides (base editors) to repair single nucleotide variants causing disease. Prime editors are available to replace short (less than 50 nucleotides) stretches of DNA to fix small insertions or deletions. Cas transpondases address larger deletions, even about 1,000 nucleotides. Other tools allow for the control of gene expression by inhibition or activation of gene expression. Similar enzymes that can even change epigenetic markers, such as histone acetylation/methylation, are now available for clinical use.

CLINICAL USES

Clinical trials are using CRISPR for somatic cell editing to treat hereditary diseases and cancers. Cells are either removed and edited in tissue culture and then reinjected into the patient, or the gene editors are packaged on viral vectors or lipid nanoparticles and given intravenously to home into specific tissues. Most ex vivo therapies (the ones that use tissue culture) have focused on two blood disorders: sickle cell disease and beta-thalassemia, both of which are caused by variation in the mutant beta globulin of human hemoglobulin. Both diseases represent evolutionary adaptations of human populations to malaria. Now that malaria is no longer a problem in certain geographic areas, such adaptations are not needed and are, in fact, detrimental to the health of the individuals who have such mutations. These new treatments are effective and lack significant side effects.

Leber congenital blindness, a disorder of the retina, has been treated by in vivo viral directed delivery of a genome editor to correct the aberrant intronic spice site CEP290 with recovery of vision: for example, one blind eight-year-old has had his vision restored to normal! Intravenous administration of lipid nanoparticles that contain CRISPR/Cas9 mRNA home to the liver to reduce liver protein production. The first indication is for transthyretin amyloidosis, in which a mutant protein causes toxic amyloid aggregations. So far, 15 patients have received CRISPR-Cas9 lipid nanoparticles to generate intels in the transthyretin gene, producing at least six months of durable editing, a decrease in serum transthyretin, and no toxic or other side effects. Wow! This is a major achievement in a disease that was previously fatal in many cases. The same technique is used to reduce kallikrein for hereditary angioedema.

CONCLUSION

A new era has dawned in which humans will control human genetics. Because all life forms on this planet, so far discovered, use the same chemistry and physiology, it is reasonable to assume that sometime in the future, humans will be able to change their brains and, if they wish, change their bodies. At some time in the future, I predict humans will be able to change their species such that a man who wished to become a dog or an elephant can do so without much trouble. All species are that similar to each other.

Changes into a plant form will also be possible for those humans who want to be a sequoia, for instance, or a rose or an eggplant. Plants and animals are that similar biologically, except plants are usually much more complicated than animals. Plants are much more sophisticated life forms than animals as measured by their instructional DNA. For instance, the instructional DNA in a pine tree is 23 times that of a human, proving the pine tree is a much more complicated living thing that a human being. Rhododendron might be an easier transformation as it has only three times the instructional DNA of a human. Also, I think it will also be possible to be a tree for a while and then revert to human status if you wish. The control of genetics will be that powerful and that universal. I, for one, have always wondered what it would be like to be a domestic house cat, and someday I may have that privilege. Composite plants are already on the scene, and many more will come in the future. So, look for mango trees making wheat and barley and look for composite humans who can breathe underwater or who have wings that enable them to fly like birds or bats. The choices and the possibilities are unlimited.

Some people will try to stop this for various reasons, just as some people tried to stop In Vitro Fertilization, cardiac catheterization, nerve block anesthesia for childbirth (the Bible says God wants women to have pain during delivery), birth control, FM Radio, antibiotics, heavier-than-air flight, vaccination for COVID-19, and so forth. Stupid people will always be with us, and some stupid ideas will have traction, especially among the stupid. Let the stupid try to stop progress. They are throwing sand against the tide.